JOIN THE ROMANCE TIME-TRAVELERS' CLUB!

Join the mailing list on mariahstone.com to receive exclusive bonuses, author insights, release announcements, giveaways and the insider scoop of books on sale - and more!

Also by Mariah Stone

CALLED BY A HIGHLANDER SERIES

Sìneag
Highlander's Captive
Highlander's Hope
Highlander's Heart
Highlander's Love
Highlander's Christmas

CALLED BY A VIKING SERIES

One Night with a Viking (prequel)—grab for free!

The Fortress of Time
The Jewel of Time
The Marriage of Time
The Surf of Time
The Tree of Time

CALLED BY A PIRATE SERIES (TIME TRAVEL ROMANCE):

Pirate's Treasure
Pirate's Pleasure

A STANDALONE REGENCY ROMANCE:

The Russian Prince's Bride

PIRATE'S TREASURE
CALLED BY A PIRATE BOOK ONE

MARIAH STONE

PIRATE'S TREASURE

A Time Travel Romance

Called by a Pirate series
Book One

Mariah Stone

This is a work of fiction. Names, characters, places, and incidents either are the products of the author's imagination or are used fictitiously. Any resemblance to actual persons, living or dead, businesses, companies, events, or locales is entirely coincidental.

© 2019 Mariah Stone. All rights reserved.

Cover design by Dar Albert

All rights reserved. This book or parts thereof may not be reproduced in any form, stored in any retrieval system, or transmitted in any form by any means—electronic, mechanical, photocopy, recording, or otherwise—without prior written permission of the publisher. For permission requests, contact the publisher at http:\\mariahstone.com

CHAPTER 1

*C*ity of Pirates Museum, Jade Island, The Bahamas, August 2019

S*amantha*

"H*e's so handsome*." I nudge my best friend, Lisa, in the ribs. "And yet he couldn't find a date for the ball."

"James 'Prince' Barrow, 1690–1720," reads the sign below the portrait of a pirate who looks like Prince Charming.

"Who wouldn't go to a ball with him, Samantha?" Lisa says. "No man can look this dreamy."

Forgetting the tour guide watching us, I roll my eyes. "I wouldn't."

James Barrow reminds me of Lisa's ex, with his pretty face and his nose held high. The conceited, arrogant, pleased-with-himself type who thinks the world belongs to him.

James Barrow's golden hair falls in soft curls to his shoulders. What color are his eyes? Blue? No, they're a bit unusual. Violet? I thought the only people with violet eyes were heroines in romance novels. It must be the artist's touch or the aging paint. Thick golden brows arch over his eyes. Today, he could be a Hollywood star or a pop singer who teenage girls secretly cry over.

Not a pirate.

"The other guy is my type," I say, pointing at the portrait hanging next to this one. Cole the Black.

He's handsome, too, but in a more brutal way. His hair long and dark, his eyes almost black under his low eyebrows—everything about him screams danger. The type of man with whom I have an understanding: no commitments, just one night of no-holds-barred, pantie-melting sex.

Between the portraits hang two identical golden necklaces with jade-stone pendants, and a note "REPLICAS" under them.

"Well, Cole the Black does look like your type, Samantha," Lisa says. "He needs someone to love his lost soul, just like you."

I snort. Lisa and her compulsion for romance. That's what got her here, so heartbroken. Just open your heart for a jerk to step on, to laugh at you, and to destroy your soul. Exactly why I'm not getting involved in anything serious anymore. It's a pain I know all too well.

Memories tighten my airways and my heart races. The heat is not helping. There's no air-conditioning, and the open windows of the building let in the scorching August air from the vastness of the Atlantic and cloudless blue sky. It smells like pear, mango, and hot stones. But I'm not complaining. The whole vacation is a pleasant contrast with New York and probably the last bit of relaxation I'll get for the next few years due to the big promotion that awaits me.

The guide raises his eyebrows in surprise and chuckles. He is a man in his sixties, local to the islands. He has a bright-red headscarf on, a simple white T-shirt, a necklace of colorful beads around his neck, and the most astonishing thing of all...

A live snake.

It slithers around his neck, its forked tongue flickering and trembling in the air. It makes my skin crawl. The man—his name is Adonis, and it must be a nickname—has assured us it's not poisonous. I am not sure I believe him. I only agreed to take the private tour in the hope that Lisa would be too distracted by the snake to think about Hank. I didn't think pirates and history would be interesting at all. So far, I've been completely wrong about both. I'm supposed to be the badass between Lisa and me, but surprisingly—or perhaps not, considering she owns a pet hotel—Lisa loves the snake. And I find the museum fascinating.

Lisa leans closer and watches the snake. She tells Adonis about her love of animals and her pet hotel in New Jersey, which has always been the source of argument between us. I wish she moved to Manhattan like I did and scored a great job. But she says she likes her hotel.

Adonis pats the snake's head, the gesture so freakish it makes my bones freeze. "Cole the Black split the bounty from their combined raid on one of the Spanish ships that transported valuables from the colonies back to Spain. Attending the governor's ball was the only way to get the last clue to the location of the treasure. James was lucky he procured the Marquis de Bouchon and his wife's invitation, but it wasn't enough. The governor's staff wouldn't have admitted him had he gone alone, and he couldn't hire a local prostitute to act as his wife," Adonis said. "The governor knew every single one, so he would have called his bluff right away. Without a woman to help James get to the ball, he never got the treasure. Tired of a sailing a long time without profit, his crew mutinied and he lost his ship. He was ready to retire, get married, buy a villa, and lead a peaceful life, but instead he was imprisoned by the Royal Navy and hanged in Bristol. His noble family was there, watching their pirate son hang."

Cold sweat trickles down my back, imagining old gray England and that gorgeous man hanging by the neck, dying. I want to yell at him to find someone, to save himself.

"So did he want the treasure to stop the mutiny?" I ask.

"Yes," Adonis says. "He had never seen piracy as the way to live forever. He even met a woman once, a pirate captain, wanted to settle down with her."

"But he didn't marry her, I assume?" I say.

"That's right." The snake turns and looks at me, its tongue darting in the air. I shiver.

"Anne betrayed him during their raid on the Spanish ship, and James had to lie low from the British Navy for a long time afterward."

"That must have broken James's heart," Lisa says.

Adonis nods. "It did. But at least Cole kept his word and hid James's part of the treasure."

"See," Lisa exclaims. "I told you, Cole was just a lost soul. He could have taken all the treasure for himself, but he didn't. He just needs love to open up his heart."

I shake my head. "I'm astonished you are still a hopeless romantic even after the breakup."

Adonis chuckles and seems to exchange a knowing look with the snake. Could he be any weirder?

"So that no one else could get the treasure," Adonis continues, "Cole created three clues to its location. The first was the island map, the second was the exact location of the treasure on the map. James found both of those. The only thing he was missing were the coordinates of the island."

A sense of adventure begins to sizzle through my blood like a drug. It's intoxicating.

"And somehow the governor got the last clue," I say.

"Yes. The governor arrested a pirate who was supposed to

give the coordinates to James. Of course, the governor didn't know exactly what he had. Cole had hidden the coordinates in a Chinese cricket box he'd picked up when he'd raided the ship of an Asian merchant."

Lisa frowns. "A cricket box? What's that?"

I know the answer to that. "It's like one of those Japanese puzzle boxes that looks like a box of solid wood, and you have to guess where to push, press, and slide to open it."

Adonis chuckles. "You are very right, madame. How do you know?"

"My grandpa was Japanese. He collected those puzzle boxes and let me play with them. I loved watching him open them."

Adonis cocks his head, and his dark eyes glimmer. "If James had been able to steal the box and get it open, maybe he would have lived a very different life."

"I wish he had found a woman who could help him," Lisa says, and Adonis seems to hide a smile.

"Was the treasure found?" I ask.

"Yes. Eventually. These two necklaces"—he points at the jade pendants—"are their replicas. Two identical necklaces, for two noble twin sisters in Spain. Cole put one in James's half and kept one for himself."

I study the necklace. It's pretty. The gold is pale, the oval jade pendant encrusted in a sunlike ornament. "Why jade?" I ask.

"They say in voodoo, jade is the gem of love, so strong that people are able to find each other anywhere. Even through time."

As he says that, the world seems to stand still—only his lips move, and the snake. A shiver runs through me, as if someone just poured a bucket of snow over my head. Find each other through time? What nonsense. And why is he looking at me like that?

I exchange a look with Lisa, and she looks as amused as I am.

Voodoo, time travel, love. Right. I want to snort, but I don't want to offend Adonis, or his pet snake…

"Would you like to try it on?" Adonis asks.

"What?" I say. "Aren't we forbidden from touching stuff in a museum?"

Adonis smiles. "Not when I am your tour guide."

Lisa looks at me. "Yeah! Why not. They are replicas anyway, right?"

He removes the necklaces and hands us one each. The metal is cool and smooth in my hands, and it starts to buzz ever slightly. No, it must be just the contrast with the heat. The jade is so pretty. It has all these shades and swirls of gorgeous green, from light to dark, probably different layers of stone from ancient times to more recent.

"Yes, just replicas," Adonis says. "Put them on. Go on."

"I don't know," I say and shake my head. I hold the necklace out to him. "What if the guard comes? Aren't we going to get into trouble?"

Adonis winks. "The guard won't come. I promise. When else will you have a chance to try on a pirate treasure?"

Lisa looks at me, I look at her and we nod to each other, barely noticeable. "All right," I say. "A fun thing to do. Something to remember in New York."

As I put the necklace on and the stone touches my rib cage, something begins to happen. It's as if the air around me contracts and pushes me from all sides. I can't breathe. The colors around me smudge, and everything is a blur.

"What's happening?" I yell and try to remove the necklace. But I can't feel my body.

All I can hear is the snake's ominous hiss.

"You are traveling back in time to help James. To return, you must put on the necklace."

This is insane!

"Lisa, don't put it on!" I yell, but I don't know if she heard me because she just stands there.

He must have put some drug on the necklace, because I feel as if the pressure is crushing me, as if I'm getting smaller and smaller, and the wind is blowing at me from all sides, and then there's a strange rocking sensation under my feet.

And then the world goes dark.

CHAPTER 2

Waters near Nassau, The Bahamas, August 1718

James

THE SUN SETTING behind the windows of my cabin lights the hand-drawn map of the island in my hand in a red-orange glow. A perfect color for the volcano indicated in the center of the island. Cole, you smart and fearless bastard. A dormant volcano is a good guard for the treasure chest.

Sea Prince rocks gently on the waves. My cabin is filled with the scent of sea and sandalwood, of the ship that has been my home for years, but that no longer *feels* like home.

I crave the scent of earth, of tropical flowers and growing things. I want to build a home on the solid ground and earn an honest living. I want the companionship of a dependable woman who won't betray me.

I do not want to look over my shoulder anymore. Do not want to court danger.

I want peace.

But it looks as though I will not get it. I do not have the island's coordinates. And without a woman to attend the ball with me tonight, I will never get them...

A sudden movement catches the corner of my eye, and I jump to my feet, whirling around, pistol in hand.

A woman lies on the floor, where a moment ago, I could swear there was empty space.

I blink and strain my eyes to make sure I am really seeing her. Was she sent to me to make my wish come true? Did God decide to smile on me? She lies on her side, one arm outstretched, her bright-yellow gown revealing the curves of her breasts. Her arms are completely nude, whereas her legs are covered almost till her feet. She's wearing strange shoes, her scandalously exposed feet held to the soles only with thin straps. Her long raven-black hair is loose and spread on the floor. Her eyes are closed, her face serene and beautiful.

Is she a spy? A thief who came looking for clues to the treasure? A prostitute hired by my crew?

"Who are you? How did you get here?" I demand.

Her eyelashes flutter. She stirs and moans a little. Then her eyes open and they're dark and deep and full of confusion. She takes in everything, as though she is seeing a different world.

"What's going on?" she mutters, her voice deep and melodic, with an American accent. She looks me over carefully, and then the meaning of a gun pointed at her seems to register. She pushes against the floor and sits up. Her eyes widen in fear, and her full lips part.

"I repeat the question," I say. "Who are you?"

She shakes her head and then raises her chin, although fear still lurks behind her eyes. "I'm Samantha Gilbert. How the hell did I get here? Did you bring me here? What do you want?"

Samantha Gilbert. She sounds so sincere, but I will be damned if I believe her. Anne taught me the lesson of never trusting beautiful women. I walk around the desk towards her and watch with satisfaction as her eyes crawl over me and she swallows. Then she frowns as though in recognition. If she is afraid, she is right to be. I will not tolerate thieves or spies on my ship, no matter how pretty.

"Miss Gilbert," I say, "I did not bring you anywhere. You came here, to me. To what do I owe the pleasure?"

She rises to her feet, and I can't help appreciating the view. She is petite and slender, the hemispheres of her breasts protruding deliciously under the freely falling material of her dress.

Whoever sent her, they chose right because she is very distracting.

And for just a fraction of a second, I lose my focus as I admire her, and she darts to the doors. But I have been trained for this, have fought battles where a moment thinner than a hair means the difference between life and death.

My hand lands on the doors just as hers reach the handle. She is panting, pinned between my body and the doors. Her scent reaches me—sun, coconut, and something citrusy. My pulse beats loudly in my ears.

I gently turn her around to face me. And as I meet her dark eyes, I have to remind myself to stay in the moment and not drown in their beauty.

"And where is it that you are going, Miss Gilbert?" I ask.

"Away from you and your gun. Where am I?" she says, her voice a croak.

I narrow my eyes, looking for any sign that she is playing me. She is an excellent actress and seems utterly sincere. But her questions do not make sense. If she came for the clues, would trying to seduce me not be a better tactic? If she is a whore, why is she behaving as though someone placed her here without her knowledge?

"If you are a jest of one of my crew," I say, "I am not laughing. It is obvious that you came for something, and are pretending—very poorly, I must say—that you lost your memory."

She shakes her head. "I'm not pretending."

"If you are a whore, which"—my gaze travels down her body, and her cheeks flush—"judging by your attire is the most likely option, I am not in the mood."

"Jesus H. Christ," she yells. "How dare you!"

"Who are you then? Who sent you?"

She swallows and looks around the room, frowns, and then her face relaxes as though in revelation. I do not care for it. She smiles and crosses her arms. They brush against my chest and send a light buzzing through my veins.

"I get it, Mr. Barrow," she says, "I just need to help you get to the ball. We find Cole's treasure. I win the escape room."

She finally admits it—she is here for the treasure. I knew it was all just a ploy. I must learn how she found out and who is behind this.

"How do you know about Cole's treasure?" I ask.

"Come on. I've been in the museum. Adonis is a great guide. You have the map of the island and the location of the treasure. Now you just need the coordinates. And to get them, you need a date. I'm your date. I can get you to the ball, Monsieur…de Bouchon if I remember correctly?"

Blood drains from my face, and I feel my lips pull into a snarl. She knows too much. She knows everything.

I put the pistol under her chin. Her smug smile is replaced with terror. She pales, her eyes as wide as saucers.

"I am asking for the last time," I say slowly, "who sent you? Think carefully about your answer. It might be the last one you ever give."

Her breath comes out in a shaky rush. "My name is

Samantha Gilbert. I was sent by Cole the Black to help you find the treasure."

"Cole is in the East Indies."

She nods. "He is. But he left me behind, just in case."

I apply more pressure to the pistol. "Prove it."

"Ehm. You need to find a Chinese cricket box at the governor's. There is a jade necklace in the treasure chest—among other things, like gold and silver and gems. You want to stop pirating, get married, and buy a villa. He told me that," she adds.

Could she possibly be telling the truth? Those were things Cole would know. No. I know a liar when I see one, and even if she knows this information, I do not believe it came from Cole. She is lying about who she is, and her sole purpose is to distract me and disorient me to get my treasure. She is as dangerous as a plague. And I am not taking any chances.

She must be isolated and put under constant guard.

I take her by the upper arm and pull her after me, opening the doors and dragging her across the deck. I ignore my crew's astonished, hungry looks at Samantha Gilbert.

She begins to struggle, and I tighten my grip. "Let me go!" she cries. "Right now. Where are you taking me?"

"To the brig. If you think I believe you, you are a fool."

CHAPTER 3

amantha

THE EYES of at least ten pirates bore into me, undress me, eat me alive.

The brig is divided into grated sections, and there's a man in one of the farther ones, also staring at me from under his eyebrows. They are all unwashed and unshaven, stinking of stale male sweat. How does James keep so clean? Oh, right, they're all just actors, I try to convince myself.

The ceilings are low and heavy beams run along them. There are no portholes. The rocking motion is stronger here, and I'm starting to get slightly seasick.

I'm admittedly terrified, somewhere deep. But I refuse to go there, because in the back of my mind, there's a voice telling me I might be in the eighteenth century. If I believe that voice, I might as well admit the existence of unicorns, elves, and dwarves. I concentrate on my anger. James, or whoever he really is, had the audacity to put me in here. I'm furious. So furious I'm shaking. He was a jerk to me. How could he just throw me in the brig with all these nasty pirates? I was right about him. Despite his charming looks, he's as vain and selfish as I thought, without a kind bone in his body. His appearance is the perfect disguise for a pirate.

I thought for sure my quick thinking would get me out of this escape-room adventure. Or whatever it is. But it's clear now that there will be no quick exit.

I guess I need to look for clues to get out of here. I close my eyes and try to calm down, try to block out the dirty pirates and think about what to do. This is not me. I don't panic. But there's something about nasty men looking at you like you're dinner that makes you freak out.

Back to rational thinking. Breathe in, breathe out. Adonis said if I want to go back, I need the jade necklace. That must be how I win this and get the hell out of this pirate insanity.

I look around, but the nausea is getting worse, and I close my eyes again and breathe—not too deeply. Cracking my eyes open, I note that the pirates are still staring at me as if I were a juicy New York steak. They are talking to one another in muffled voices, chuckling, pointing at me. Their glances are like filthy fingers touching me without permission. I've never felt so disgusted in my life.

I shiver, wrapping my arms around my chest to cover anything I can, and turn my back to them.

"Hiya, molly," someone says next to me—too close—and I turn around.

One of the men is pinned to the bars, holding the grating with both hands. He's middle-aged, bald, has bad teeth and a shaggy beard.

"What did ye do to make the cap'n dump ye here?" he says. "He dinnae like the shag?"

I've had my share of being hit on by drunk guys in bars. But none of them were so revolting, and none of them had openly suggested I was a prostitute. And I had never been trapped with so many of them. My feet and arms are heavy, my pulse drums in my ears.

I begin to look for some sort of a trap door in the floor, running my fingers against the old, chipped wood.

"Nae, how could ye not like the shag when a molly sports dairies like that," another man joins in, standing beside the first. He's smaller and rounder, but he's actually drooling, looking at my chest. I think he means my breasts. Prickling heat spreads through my cheeks and my neck. I'm not a saint, but oh my gosh! I wish the floor would open and swallow me whole. I've never felt like this, as dirty as a floor mat.

Man, I'd love to kick this guy's ass.

If this were really an escape room, there must be a way out. But the floor is just a floor. I stand up and study the wall. They smell like seawater and tar, and there's not a single indent or crack to indicate a secret door or give me a clue how to get out. This is starting to seem pretty extreme for a museum.

"Yeah"—a third man joins, and the rest of them follow to stand behind the grating in a dark wall of grimy faces—"she looks like a good shag."

I've had enough. "Okay," I say. "Now that we've all established that I would be a good *shag*, can we please move on with our day, guys?"

As if I hadn't made a sound, the first guy turns to the rest of them. "How long since ye had yerself a molly?"

They shrug and mutter. "Probably as long as ye," says the third pirate.

They all turn to me again, but clearly they are talking to one another. "Do ye think the cap'n would mind?" says another one.

They study me, contemplating.

"Even if he would, he ain't goin' to be cap'n for long," says someone, but without any confidence in his voice.

Right, the possible mutiny. James needs the treasure to stop his crew from overthrowing him.

"Go away, all of you," I yell. I know the guy who plays James would not want them to have a go with me. "I'm not for the taking. Shut up and stop looking at me. Go away."

They listen, shocked, then erupt in laughter. "Feisty," says one of them and nods in appreciation. "A bit of fire in ye, eh?"

"Who has the key?" someone asks.

Now that sobers me up like a cold shower. I frantically look around. Maybe I'm meant to have the key in my cell? It's one thing to tolerate this stupid game when they are behind the grating. It's another to have to physically fight them off.

"Cap'n," says one of them, and they all sigh in disappointment.

"But there's a spare," says another.

No!

"Where?"

"Mr. Killian has it."

"Ah, the quartermaster, of course. Go fetch it then. What are ye waiting for."

One of them separates from the crowd and climbs the stairs.

"I'll scream," I say.

They guffaw. "Told ye, feisty," one of them says.

"Dibs on the first round," says the pirate who came to the cell first. "I like 'em fresh and juicy."

One of the big ones standing at the back shoves him. "What makes ye think ye can call dibs? I like 'em fresh and juicy, too. She'll lose all her fire after a couple of ye."

Now cold sweat breaks through my skin for real. I don't think I ever felt that. Even in nightmares. "You fuckers," I mutter. "If one of you lays a finger on me, you'll be missing it."

"Then Mr. Finn should have the first go," a man at the back says. "His plug tail is no bigger than a pinkie."

They all erupt in laughter, making me shiver. Only the first pirate doesn't laugh.

"No. She's mine," he says. "Where's that key?"

As he says that, the men stop laughing and begin to quarrel. Quickly, it gets loud. Their faces are furious, and they're shoving one another, yelling. The first guy grabs the grate and starts shaking it, his eyes bulging, his mouth a snarl.

Trembling now, I retreat several steps until my back is pressed against the wall. My throat clenches so tight I feel as if someone is choking me. More men descend the stairs and join the mob. The very air—heavy with moisture and smelling of bad breath, rum, and unwashed bodies—is charged with aggression. Then the fight starts...

As men punch and kick one another, I crawl into the corner and squeeze my eyes tightly closed. This is not an escape room. This must be a dream. A nightmare. Wake up, I tell myself. *Wake up!*

Then a deafening bang rends the air, and the smell of something acrid and burned reaches my nose. It's suddenly quiet. So quiet I hear my ears ringing.

Maybe the nightmare is over.

One, two, three. I open my eyes.

I'm still in the cell, surrounded by filthy, horny pirates, but the actor who plays James Barrow has his pistol pointed at them. There's so much power in his gaze, my knees melt.

Next to him stands another man, older, with two pistols in his hands. But their barrels are directed towards the floor. It's a warning not a confrontation.

"What's the source of this?" "James" demands. I'm simply going to call him James in my head, I decide. His voice is calm but steely.

They are quiet for a few moments, then the guy who came to my cell first says, "The molly."

James glances at me, worry in his eyes, and I stand up, letting him know I'm all right. My legs and arms are still shaky.

"What did she do?" he asks.

He didn't seriously just assume *I* did something. I knew he was full of himself. "What? Typical man... Always blame the woman first. I didn't do a thing."

He shoots a quick glance at me, and the pirates start to yell. The room fills with noise again, and they stab their hands in my direction.

"We were just deciding who gets the first go at her," says one of the pirates.

James's face straightens, his violet eyes dark. "What?"

The whole room is so silent, we can hear the muffled splashes of the waves against the ship.

"Ain't she—"

"I'm not a prostitute, you jerk," I yell.

"But she's dressed— Those dairies—"

James's lip crawls up into a snarl. His eyes glow with fury. "If she were a whore, I'd have told you. She is just a prisoner. Under my protection."

Under his protection... The words make my chest feel lighter. I've never been under anyone's protection. Not even the first man I ever loved said that to me.

A rumble goes through the crew, but it stays low, then dies.

James continues. "I put her here because she might be a thief. A spy. Because she might disrupt our discipline and get what she's after. The same thing you and I are after. The treasure."

They are completely quiet now. Looking guilty as naughty dogs.

"Sorry, Cap'n," says the first pirate who wanted to plunder me, then glances at me. "She looks like a spy. Distracting with her dairies like that."

James purses his lips angrily. "I've made a mistake. I had

thought it would be safe to keep her here, away from my cabin. But I was wrong."

He moves towards my cage and his crew gives way. I breathe easier now. His gaze finds mine, and my heart skips a beat.

Goddamn.

He turns the key in the hole and my heart beats again, faster this time. He opens the door and holds his hand to me.

"Even if you are a spy or a thief, it seems the safest place for you is with me," he says.

His violet eyes glow in the golden light of the torches, looking right into my soul.

And what I see is hope.

I take a few steps and place my hand in his. Mine is all clammy from sweat and cold. His is warm and dry and strangely reassuring.

"Come, Miss Gilbert," he says, and his gaze melts my insides. "It seems we have a ball to attend."

CHAPTER 4

ames

I SHUT the doors of my cabin behind me and study Miss Gilbert's back. I am still seething after what happened downstairs. This beautiful, brave, stubborn woman with raven hair and eyes as deep and dark as hell had almost caused a mutiny.

Though it is not her I am angry with. It is myself.

Tonight is the only chance I have to get the last clue, and I am desperate, distracted. I did not think of the consequences of putting her in the brig, dressed like that, and underestimated the tension in my crew. They have not been ashore for a month now, and are itching for spoils—and for women.

Miss Gilbert—Samantha—turns to face me, her eyes wide. Damnation, look at her. The flawless skin, the elegant arches of her eyebrows, the soft lips that call for a kiss. Any man would feel tempted.

She is hugging herself protectively, but her chin is high. A proud woman with a backbone. I cannot help but be impressed.

But what am I doing, worrying about how she feels? She is not my responsibility, and I ought not feel anything for her but suspicion. I still do not know who she really is. Her story about being sent by Cole is too convenient. After Anne, I cannot trust another woman.

"Your coworkers went a little too far downstairs, don't you agree?" she says. "I want to go. It's hard to imagine that your museum bosses will be too happy after I complain. I've had enough adventures today. I want to go back to my hotel."

Is she speaking in code words that I ought to understand? Another piece of Cole's puzzle, perhaps?

"Museum bosses?" I say.

She gestures to the ceiling with one arm. "Don't you have someone you report to?"

I roll my shoulders back, her words making my neck muscles as tense as ropes at storm, just like they had always been in Bristol. "I did not become a pirate to report to anyone. If I wanted someone to run my life, I would have stayed in England, run the company alongside my father, and led the life my family had in sight for me."

The day Cole and I had decided to become pirates, to end the tyranny of the captain of my father's trade ship, had been the happiest day of my life.

She shakes her head. "Listen, buddy, that's enough. I know you're an actor. I want to get off this ship and go back to my hotel. Actually, scratch that. Back to New York. I've had enough Caribbean vacations for now."

Bloody hell, the nerve of her. An actor? I cannot remember anyone talking to me like that, trying to tell me what to do. Not since Anne. Blood boils in my veins, hot and prickly. I leave the doors and walk towards her, my fists clenched. "You will go back to New York when *I* allow it."

She gasps as I lean over her, and her eyes darken.

"You will help me get the cricket box," I say. "Just as you claimed you came for."

She groans. "Are you seriously still playing this? You are going to be in so much trouble once this is over." She stabs her index finger at me, and I want to bend her over my knee. "I'll sue you. Personally. You'll be sorry you didn't let me go. Is there like a safe word or something? Because I'm done."

I chuckle. My anger is gone, replaced by curiosity. She is a mystery. Graceful in her appearance and movements but graceless in her manner of expression. She cannot be pure nobility. I like that because nobility bores me. "Sue me? Are you threatening to woo me? That sounds intriguing."

She throws her hands up, turns around, and hides her face in them. Either she is acting or she is truly dismayed. The urge to comfort her, to wrap my arms around her shoulders, makes my hands itch.

"Miss Gilbert." I take a step towards her.

She sighs and turns around, her eyes cold. "All right, mister." She straightens her back. "If the only way to get out of here is to play your stupid game, I'll play it. What's next? The ball?"

She is charming in her anger, and something deep in her eyes tells me she is not pretending, but I refuse to believe that. She looks both helpless and resolved. The woman has strength.

Even more reason not to trust her. "First, Miss Gilbert, I must insist that you tell me who you really are."

She rolls her eyes, then pinches the bridge of her nose and keeps silent for a few moments. "I am the daughter of a merchant from New York. Cole the Black raided our ship on the way to Jamaica and took my friend hostage. I'm very worried about her and I need to help you get the treasure so that he lets her go."

I frown. This sounds like something he would do. "But you agreed he is in the East Indies."

"Yes. He sailed away with her and hired a boat to get me to you. But the captain made advances towards me, and so I'm left in this." She gestures down at her body.

I clench my jaws. "How will he find out that you were successful?"

"You need to give me the jade necklace so that I can find him and show it to him. Once he sees it, he'll know you got the treasure, and he'll let my friend go."

I scoff. "You are not seriously hoping you'll get anything from the treasure chest."

"I just need that necklace. The rest is yours."

I shake my head, both amazed and astonished by her audacity. She is stirring something in me, feelings I buried two years ago, and I must stop them.

To do that, I must plunge myself into activity. The ball. It is high time we go. I walk towards the door to my private quarters. "You are asking for the necklace when you are completely in my power? You ought to be grateful that you are going to make it off my ship alive and in one piece, considering your life rests in the hands of a pirate. Now, come. We must get you dressed."

I open the door and turn to her. She is watching me with raised eyebrows. "I can dress myself."

She must feel shy. "Miss Gilbert, although I am enjoying very much seeing you dressed like this, you cannot go to the ball in your undergarments. Therefore, I am afraid I am your only option to get the corset and the dress on. There are no women on my ship apart from you. And surely you do not want any of my crew to help you?"

A blush covers her cheeks, her nostrils flare, and she straightens her back. "I don't need you."

A smile spreads my lips. "Did you grow a pair of arms on your back?"

She frowns. "Of course not."

I gesture for her to enter my private quarters, and the thought of her in my quarters—in my bed—sets my blood on fire. "Then you need me," I say, and my voice comes out huskier than I intended.

She swallows and licks her lips, then walks past me, and her scent tickles my nostrils and stirs desire in me.

Inside the cabin, I look in one of the sea chests for Anne's attire. The silk of the jade dress she wore *that* day is gentle against my rough fingers. Pain stabs me at the memory of the day I met her three years ago.

I was walking with Cole to meet the local plantation owner to sell the plunder we had raided. Every pair of male eyes turned somewhere, and when I followed them, my heart stopped. I saw that silk sweeping the pavement of Nassau as she walked with her parasol. Her hair shone like a freshly minted gold coin in an exquisite hairdo, her amber eyes big and innocent, watching everything around her as if she were in a wondrous French garden, not among pirates, whores, and smugglers.

Something took me over then. Maybe I wanted to protect her. Maybe I just wanted *her*. Breaking all etiquette towards a lady, I approached her. That very evening on my ship, in that bed, I found out that she was no lady.

Later I found out that she had an even bigger ship than me. And even later, that she was still married and all she needed was to give me to the British so that she and her husband, the famous pirate Samuel van Huisen, would get a pardon.

"This is pretty. Whose is it?" Miss Gilbert asks.

My fingers tighten around the material, and I stand up holding the dress out to her. As I look into her face, I wonder what hides behind those eyes. She's strong, bold, and smart. Beautiful. A storm starts roaring in my blood, and I realize I am in danger of repeating the same mistake again. No doubt, she is here for my treasure. "A woman who is long dead," I say.

She frowns but takes the dress. As she does, our fingers touch, and fire runs through my veins like a lightning strike. Our eyes lock. Her lips part, and the need to taste them scorches me.

No. Not another woman like that. I let go of the dress and sink to my knees to find the undergarments for her, but the silkiness of the thin shift and stockings, and an image of removing them slowly from her luscious limbs, spreads the raging tempest through parts of my body best ignored. I shove the items to her before I can act on my desires and gesture towards the french screen.

She walks there and disappears behind it. I hear the whisper of clothes against her skin as she takes them off.

Glimpses of Miss Gilbert's bare flesh flashing through the gaps between the panels only make me burn hotter. I yearn to see her whole, to touch her, to kiss her.

To have her.

I cannot stop looking. Through the gaps between the screens, the curve of her waist teases me, the full side of her breast gives rise to a low growl that originates deep in my gut and that I stop before it exits my lips. The round cheek of her gorgeous behind almost makes me reach out to grab her.

No.

I turn around to face the wall. I'm steaming. My cock is swelling, heavy with need.

"James?" she says after a while.

Dear Lord. If she is going to ask me to join her, I will not say no. "Yes, Miss Gilbert."

"I have the shift and the stockings on. I guess the corset is next?"

I swallow as the images of her naked body, writhing, moaning, sliding beneath me flash through my mind. I want to throw myself at her like a wild animal. Slowly, I turn around.

The sight of her standing in the white shift and stockings,

holding the corset before her, kicks the air out of me. My heart stops. These undergarments cover more of her than the yellow shift, but seeing her in them feels more erotic. Maybe because they're so common. So normal. Something I am craving.

A home.

Her eyes lock with mine, and I sink into them. Her lips are soft and red and calling for me.

I take the corset out of her hands. "Turn around."

A gentleman should not know how to lace a corset, but I am no gentleman. Not quite.

I wrap the corset around her thin waist and feel her breasts sink into it. They must be soft and silky. I tie the laces at her back—I've done it for lovers before. I avoid studying the delicate curve of her neck under her thick, glossy hair, the gentle movements of her muscles under the thin material of the shift. Samantha Gilbert must be the most beautiful woman I have ever seen.

When I finish tying the laces, her waist is perfectly narrow and straight—as if she needs any help there. And the sight of her sweet, round, delicious behind makes my fingers itch to touch, to pull her back against my pulsating erection.

I reach for the panniers and help her attach them, then take the dress she had hung over the french screen.

I just need to endure this evening. As soon as she gets me the clue, I'll leave her in Nassau, get the treasure, start a new life, and forget about her.

But as she takes the dress from my hands and begins to put it on, I freeze, mesmerized by the sight. It looked like a costume on Anne, like she had always played a role in it. On Samantha, it looks as though it was meant for her all along. She pulls the sleeves on and now the only thing left to do is to lace the dress up her back, which I do, the warmth of her body burning my fingertips through the fabric. When she turns around, everything stands still.

The fabric cups her breasts and highlights her tiny waist. The color complements her dark hair and creamy skin, and as she watches me, her cheeks begin to blush, and her eyes shine.

She is so gorgeous it hurts to look at her, and I do not think that I will ever forget the sight.

I realize in that moment that I am in serious danger of losing everything, of smiling foolishly after her as she walks away with both the treasure and my heart.

CHAPTER 5

*N*assau, New Providence Island, The Bahamas, later that evening

SAMANTHA

AS JAMES HELPS me out of the small boat, a close look at the shore of Nassau hits me like a wrecking ball. I was already suspicious in the boat on the way from the ship to the shore, as there were no lights on the island. I had a few calm minutes to think while two sailors rowed and James stared at the shore. A million questions began popping in my head. How did I get on the ship? Clearly, I had been wrong about it being an escape room. Had Adonis drugged me and kidnapped me? He'd said something about time travel, but it couldn't be *actual* time travel, could it?

Now, standing in the place where last night there were cruise ships, yachts, luxury hotels, and cute colorful houses, I see no quay, no asphalt roads, no electric lights. Instead, at the end of a wooden pier, a horse-drawn carriage awaits us, lit by torches with real fire…

As James and I walk down the pier, I know that this is not an escape room, an escape ship, or even an escape park. It is in fact the craziest, wildest explanation of all: I traveled back in time.

And oh my God, what about Lisa? Did she travel back in time, too? No, she couldn't have possibly put on that necklace after she saw me disappear. I have to believe she stayed back in the twenty-first century.

The thought that I have left everyone and everything I know shocks me so much, that I stop walking. The wooden jetty shifts under my feet. The corset squeezes me and bites into my flesh. I can't breathe. Sweat breaks through my skin. I'm too hot. The exotic scents of a tropical island—mango and sea—are too heavy, too thick. I want the smells of gas and the subway, of strong coffee and street falafel. I want to go back to New York.

I double up, my hands on my knees, and breathe. James sinks into a squat in front of me, his violet eyes filled with concern. Darn it he's handsome.

Adonis's voice talks in my head. *You are traveling back in time to help James. To return, you must put on the necklace.*

"Are you all right, Miss Gilbert?" James says. "Did I tighten your corset too much?"

I swallow, the combination of my realization and the look of concern in his eyes is disorienting. Should I tell him I came from the future? No, it's probably not a good idea. Not yet, anyway. He still doesn't trust me. And he would think I'm a lunatic. If I want to go back to my time, I need to get the treasure even more than he does. Making him think I'm crazy won't help.

I straighten and take a deep breath. He stands up as well.

"I'm all right," I say. "The dress is a little tight, that's all."

His eyes crawl down my body and darken. I get even warmer. "Would you like me to loosen the corset?"

Where did the arrogant, self-absorbed jerk go? His voice caresses me, and my bones become melted caramel. When I was changing behind the french screen, I thought he was watching me, and a buzz had run through my skin. When his fingers had brushed against me as he was tying up the corset, all of my senses seemed to focus in on the touch. His fingers had sent sweet charges of current through me, making me feel as though I were getting deliciously drunk. Warmth had spread over my skin, and every hair on my body had stood up.

I had hoped he would stop tying up the laces and release them instead.

But he hadn't. He'd just helped me dress. Although, his eyes had shifted from violet to amethyst and burned in the glow of candlelight.

If he touches me again, I'm not sure we'll make it to the party. "No," I say. "I'm better. Let's go."

As we continue our walk, my legs feel weaker, and my previous bravado disappears. What if we don't get the coordinates? What if someone recognizes James and I'm considered guilty by association? What if now James and I both hang as pirates?

I need to be very, very careful.

James shows the invitation to the coachman, and we climb into the carriage. We are silent on the way, as I gaze out of the window still digesting my recent realization. We pass by the streets of the old town. If I had any doubts before, they completely vanish now that I see the state of the buildings. The streets are full of sailors, prostitutes, and merchants, many of them wearing dirty clothes, all from the eighteenth century. It smells like rum and grilled meat.

I think I feel James's eyes on me, studying me. As we leave the town and drive into the darkness of nature, the landscape changes from savanna to occasional tropical trees and bushes.

James says, "You have been pale ever since we got ashore. Are you feeling unwell?"

I meet his gaze, and the sight of him calms me down a little. He is probably my only hope to get back. I have never depended on a man like this in my life.

And he's not the Prince Charming I thought he was.

I am in the presence of a real bad boy. And the thought makes me see him with different eyes.

"Yes," I say. "I guess I was just a little seasick on the way. Is it going to be long until we reach the governor's estate?"

"Should not be long."

After some time, we stop at the gates to a pale-yellow mansion with tall columns. There are white balustrades around the large porch and a wraparound balcony above. Tall windows shine from both floors, and two square towers flank the front porch with a wide staircase. The path to the mansion is lit with torches on both sides, and a sprawling garden stretches into the darkness around the house.

James helps me get out of the carriage. He takes my hand, and his warm, slightly calloused skin burns me. He's gallant, his back straight, his face the cold social mask of a nobleman. Where did the pirate go? He's still dangerous, but now there's something more about him. As I step down from the carriage, our eyes lock, and the ground under my feet seems to drop away for a moment.

The air is thick and slightly humid, dampening my brow as we walk down the gravel path of the garden. Through the lit windows, I see people in period clothing walking, talking, and drinking from crystal glasses. Classical music plays quietly in the background.

Placing my hand on his arm as we walk towards the house, James says, "We are newlyweds. The marquis owns plantations on Cuba, and the governor wants to sell him some of his land on Nassau."

"How did you get the invitation in the first place?"

James's voice is cool as he says, "I stole it before it even reached the marquis. I had it from a reputable source that the governor has never met the marquis and knows little about the man. So your mission is to charm the governor and distract him while I look for the cricket box. It must be in his study."

"No way. I'm coming with you."

"No, you are not, madame. You are to ensure no one notices that I slip away."

The only thing I need to ensure is that I come with him to the island. I open my mouth to argue when I notice that we're at the bottom of the stairs and that two servants standing by either side of the grand doors are looking at us. My mind is racing, trying to remember all of the period dramas I have ever watched. How did people behave back then? Should I curtsy? No, they are servants. But probably before the governor. Or maybe just the queen?

James leads me up the stairs and gives one of the servants an envelope with a broken seal. The servant nods, opens the letter, and takes it inside. From the gap in the door, music and people's voices grow louder and my heart begins to pound. My God! What if I behave so strangely I give both myself and James away? My mouth stiffens as if I'm having a spasm.

"Marquis de Bouchon." The servant returns. "The governor is surprised to see you. He thought you had left Nassau."

Oh damn. James's arm tightens under my hand, and his face turns stony. "The governor must be mistaken."

He forgot the French accent. The servant's eyebrows snap together.

My skin is prickling. Is that it? This can't be it. James is turning white, his hand reaching for the back of his pants where I know he hid a pistol.

I must do something, or we'll lose everything.

"I asked my husband to stay for the ball," I blurt out, mimicking a French accent as best I can.

The servant holds my gaze and studies me. "Of course, madame." He cocks his head.

He opens the door blinding me a little with the wash of light. Are we in?

There are beautiful ladies in similar dresses to mine and gentlemen dressed like James. Some wear white wigs. Classical music plays louder now, some sort of high-pitched piano. A man by the door looks directly at us and gives a short bow. Judging by his less impressive clothing than the rest of the guests, I think he's another servant.

James leads me through the doors. His hand is warm and steady and reassuring, and that's good because my knees are getting a little wobbly as I try to get my head around the fact that I'm in the middle of a freaking ball in 1718.

"Marquis de Bouchon and Marquise de Bouchon," the man exclaims for the whole room to hear, and all eyes are on us.

Do we bow? Do I curtsy? James stands still, and so do I. My heart beats so hard against my rib cage, it might break the bones.

An older man in rich clothes and a white wig comes to us, a girl in her late teens by his side.

"Marquis and Marquise." The man gives a small bow, and James follows suit.

The girl curtsies. I do, too, hoping I got it right. The man studies us, his eyes cold. There's a polite wariness in his gaze. This must be Governor Richardson and his daughter.

"Welcome," the governor says.

I gather the skirts of my beautiful jade dress, but underneath them my legs shake. I step farther into the room full of eighteenth-century aristocrats, a woman from the future on the arm of a pirate disguised as Prince Charming.

CHAPTER 6

amantha

INSIDE, the air is warm and stuffy, body odor is thick, mixed with a heavy rose-and-vanilla scent. Ladies fan themselves. Some of their wigs must be bigger than their heads and just as heavy. I'm glad James and I managed a tasteful hairdo that doesn't look like a bird's nest on top of my head.

The room is full of people and hums with voices and occasional eruptions of laughter. Before James can start a conversation with the governor, a servant appears next to the man and whispers something in his ear, and the governor excuses himself. I breathe easier now that we don't need to talk to him, and I exchange a glance with James. The muscles around his eyes relax, and I think he's relieved, too, although it's hard to say what lies behind his stonelike social profile. Was he like this as a young boy in Bristol? Servants with trays of drinks stand all over the room, and James takes two glasses of dark-red liquid and brings one to me.

He takes a sip and so do I. It's a delicious port wine, and it's cool. I wonder how they managed that in this heat. With the stress of the last few hours, I gulp the whole glass down in the hopes it'll help loosen me up a little. James raises his eyebrows, probably at my bad manners, but I don't care.

People are staring at us, and there's a man standing with a big sketchbook quickly moving his pencil, throwing glances in my direction. Is he the paparazzi of the time?

Through the open doors to another room, a different style of music begins to play, this time a violin and a harpsichord. It sounds like Mozart or Beethoven or something. People are going into the room, and James leads me there, too. His steady arm, through which I thread my hand, feels stable and reassuring.

People stand along the walls of the room. It's very pretty—teal-paneled walls, paintings of the Caribbean landscape, pale-teal curtains with golden ornaments. The furniture is elegant, all French style.

We stand by the wall and I lean to James. "So, how do we get to the study?"

"You need to distract Richardson, and I will find it."

"How do you suggest I distract him?" I ask, eyeing the governor as he talks to a woman in her fifties.

"Dance with him."

The muscles on my face go slack as I stare at James. "What?"

He frowns. "A minuet. Why are you acting so surprised, Miss Gilbert? Dancing is a usual practice at balls. Can you not dance?"

I'm watching the couples who are walking rather than dancing in the sense that I am used to. They are moving in Z patterns, turning, circling, strolling sideways while holding hands. It all looks very complex.

"I'm out of practice," I say.

"Let me refresh your memory then." He offers me his hand. "We shall do the next one."

My mouth goes as dry as sand. Dance a minuet in the room full of people who are staring at me? I mean, I love music. I took salsa classes, and I pick up the moves pretty fast. But this? "I…"

"What?"

"I'll just talk to him. I don't need to dance with him."

"No. You do. This is the best way to ensure he's occupied. Stopping in the middle is highly impolite and the last thing he would do."

He glances at me and his face softens. He finds my hand hidden in the folds of the skirt and squeezes it reassuringly.

"Especially with a beautiful woman like yourself. He shall be enslaved by your charm."

My heart pounds in my chest. For a moment, the dark steel wall in his eyes lifts, and I glimpse into him. And there's not a trace of arrogance or selfishness. I see kindness and support. I see the edge of vulnerability—a man who was hurt, who is desperate for a change and realizes he holds the last chance to turn his life around.

I recognize a lot of that in myself. "Okay," I say. "Let's do this."

* * *

James

I TAKE Miss Gilbert's hand, and it is cool and smooth and soft. A surge of energy runs underneath my skin, caressing me. Our eyes lock, and I feel her insecurity, her hesitation. Something is worrying her, and I have the urge to support her, to give her the steady hand that she needs right now.

This seems to be untypical of her. She gave me the impression of a woman who does not need anyone's permission to say or do what she wants. The kind of woman I admire.

Like Anne.

Anne who betrayed me.

Would Samantha do the same?

The warm, pleasant waves radiating from her touch tell me no. And I do not know if I want to believe that impulse. All I need her for is the third clue. Not an eternity together.

As Samantha and I walk towards the ballroom to take our positions, we breathe as one, walk in the same stride. She is watching the current dancers, her eyes wide, worry written on her face. Her skin is so smooth, and her touch creates a lightning storm between our fingers.

Good God, if this is how I feel when we are just holding hands, how would it feel to have her underneath me, her legs around me? How would it feel to plunge into her depths?

An eternity later, or maybe just a second, the music stops, and the couples assume their positions. I lead Samantha onto the dance floor, and sheer panic crosses her face. Did she really forget how to dance? Did she never learn how?

No, she must remember. I have not danced since I was in Bristol, an adolescent still, but my body remembers. I also remember the candles in brightly lit ballrooms, the scent of sweat masked with perfume, my mother's strict glances following me. She was trying, already then, to find a beneficial match for me, a bride from a family as rich as my parents and of the same or higher social status. I remember my father always talking with his business peers with a stern face. That whole life was about duty. Pirate life was about freedom. Now I need something in between.

I return my mind to Samantha, an explanation born in my head. She is likely completely out of practice, and I must help her. The urge to save beautiful women in distress is my weakness. I catch her dark eyes with mine. Standing across the dance floor, her dark hair gleaming, pale skin glowing against the jade fabric, she looks like a vision out of place and time. And it is as if everyone else in the room fades to black and white.

Her hands shake and her chest rises and falls quickly. "I will not let you fall," I mouth to her and give her a slow nod.

Somehow, she understands me. Her face softens and relaxes, she takes a deep breath and manages a smile. Something connects us as we look at each other, as though invisible strings stretch out between us.

The music plays, the ladies curtsy, the gentlemen bow.

And we begin.

One by one, the couples come together, curtsy, and join hands. Then they turn and walk forward together. When our turn comes, and her hand is finally in mine, I fly high as a sea bird.

I do not see anyone but her, I do not hear anything but the music, and I do not feel anything but her skin against mine. I lead her. I know I am her lighthouse, and her movements become mine, mine hers. Her hand is warm and smooth, sending gentle waves of sunshine through me. We are in the rhythm, and I feel when she gives in, her body now attuned to mine.

God Almighty, I enjoy it so much.

It reminds me of home, of being part of a family. The family I want to have. My mother threw balls like these at our house, and I was allowed to stay late and dance to practice my social skills as future heir, even though I was still an adolescent. I remember the lightness and curiosity and excitement, meeting new people, dancing with grown women. The feeling of comfort and being carefree.

This is what I want. Not a life of hiding and looking over my shoulder. But a full life that I can share with someone I am proud to call my wife. Someone who will never betray me. Someone dependable.

I look at Samantha, and right at this moment, I imagine such a life with her. Silly, but my heart sings.

We dance sideways and then meet diagonally again, hands touching, and turn. Then we go back to the corners again. Every time our hands connect, I brush one finger against the inside of her palm playfully. I want to show her that I am with her and that she is dancing extraordinarily well. The gesture is secret, and the special way her eyes shine makes me hide a smile. I have not felt this relaxed and happy in a long time. And I want the dance to last forever.

We repeat the patterns several times, together even when we are apart, as if no one and nothing else makes sense but the two of us. She does not make every movement correctly, but she brings something of her own into the dance—her natural grace and flexibility and playfulness. In her movements, there is vulnerability, another glimpse into who she is. Kind, romantic, and young.

The music comes to an end, and we stop, back where we started. I bow. She curtsies. And I want to cross the dance floor, pick her up, and kiss her. The clothes are constrictive, I want—I need—to feel what we just had, skin to skin. I want to dissolve in her.

But I do not move. I do not breathe. She does not, either. The room is dark around us. Only she is in light, and I feel as if I am a moth, helplessly drawn towards her.

* * *

SAMANTHA

I NOTICE, painfully, that everyone is staring at us. The rest of the couples left the dance floor, and it's just us. I look around, wanting to cover myself. I hate that so many people just witnessed the deepest, strangest, most spiritual connection I've ever had with a human being.

The dance showed me what it's like to have a partner who has my back. No man has ever had my back. This one does. Fear claws at the corner of my heart. Fear of being too vulnerable, of showing him the real me, of starting to care about him...

But I don't allow it to go deeper.

This is how Lisa thinks, I remind myself. Naive, romantic Lisa. I don't need a man to feel supported and complete. All I need men for is sex. Which makes me think...if James and I were so perfect in a dance, would we be as perfect in bed?

I think I'd like to find out.

He's not the arrogant jerk I thought he was. He looks younger here, in this moment, and I can see the gentleman he once was before he became a pirate. Kind. Playful. A dreamer.

He comes to me and offers his hand, and as I put mine in his, I feel like I've arrived back home.

As we join the guests standing along the walls, the next round of dancers takes the floor, and the governor is among them. He's about to dance with the lady I saw him talking to.

I sigh with relief. "I don't think I need to dance with him, James. Look."

He nods, and devils are playing in his eyes. "Come with me, then."

And as we walk out through the french doors into the garden, the tropical air caresses my heated cheeks. James pulls me deeper into the garden, then he stops and pins me to a tree trunk, one arm braced above my head. His face is gorgeous in the shadows, and I think he must be the most handsome man I've ever seen.

There's so much heat in his eyes my skin blazes. He's breathing heavily and watching me. I wrap my hands around his neck and pull him to me. His lips come so close I can smell the port on his breath, mixed with something delicious that's his alone. The combination so intoxicating, I feel drunk.

But just before his lips can touch mine, his eyes harden. He bows his head and slowly pulls away.

My heart beats against my ribs. My stomach twists with disappointment and the pain of rejection.

James frowns, his lips a thin line.

"There is no time for distraction, Miss Gilbert," he says, and without another word he turns and walks back towards the house.

He is an arrogant, conceited jerk after all.

CHAPTER 7

*S*amantha

My legs are still a little shaky as I follow James through the dark garden. My stomach is so tight it hurts, and my cheeks are burning from embarrassment. I can't even look at him as he walks ahead of me in the darkness. I'm not looking for a declaration of love, but he could have acknowledged that he's attracted to me. His withdrawal stings so much I'm dizzy. It reminds me of Leo, and I hate that. The naive girl I used to be, who wanted a soul mate and romance, is long gone. If I didn't need James, this is where *I* would be long gone.

But I need that jade necklace. So he's very mistaken if he thinks we'll go our separate ways once we get the cricket box.

Music flows out of the lit, open windows from the rooms where the ball is fully underway. James and I circle the house until we find some dark windows. We peer into them. There's a library, then a sitting room. Finally, one room has a desk, bookshelves, and chairs.

"This must be the study," James says.

The window is closed. He pushes it, then pulls at the sides to force it open but can't. I pick up a tree branch the gardeners must have missed. If he can't to the job, I will. We are getting inside one way or another.

"Get back," I say.

James frowns at me and his eyes widen as he sees the branch in my hands. "No, the noise…"

"No one is going to hear anything with the music and so many people chatting. Come on, get back."

He scowls and stretches out his hand. "Allow me."

I smirk and hand him the branch. "Oooh, what a gentleman."

His jaw muscles tighten, and I see his muscles bulge as he assumes the position to break the window. "Trust me, Miss Gilbert, I am no gentleman."

He hits the glass and it shatters. He carefully puts his arm through the hole and opens the window. He gets in first and offers his hand to help me, but I ignore him and climb over the windowsill—awkwardly, with all these layers. His face darkens, but he doesn't say anything, just walks to the table and lights a candle.

As my feet touch the parquet, I look around. Across the room is the door to the hallway. Bookshelves line one wall, and there's a desk to the right with a big globe next to it. Landscape paintings hang on the other walls. It smells sweet and a little musty, like books, dust, and wood. The music from the ball is faint, muffled by the walls and doors.

I breathe out. After hours in this corset and dress—and after the boat, the dancing, the almost kiss—I'm suddenly hyper-aware of how uncomfortable I am. The corset digs into my flesh and suffocates me. I feel claustrophobic and claw at the back of my dress in a futile attempt to loosen the laces. "God, where did you find this dress anyway?" I mumble. James is going through the drawers of the desk with one hand, holding the candle in the other.

Then it hits me. "A woman who is long dead," he'd said.

"Wait. Did this dress belong to Anne?" I ask. He looks as if I just drove a knife into his chest.

"How do you know about Anne?" he asks, his voice coarse.

Oh damn.

"Cole told me," I say. I'm going to make him hate Cole, aren't I?

"Why would he tell you about Anne?"

"Well…" I look around the room to distract myself from unpleasant images of James and another woman. I need to busy myself with searching for the box. "It came up." I walk to a bookshelf. "Is it, though? Anne's?"

"Not that it concerns you in any way. But yes, it is."

My eyes are darting through the rows of books. *Small wooden box, look for a small wooden box.*

"She must have looked stunning in it," I say. *Small goddamn wooden box.* Why did I need to ask about the woman he loved? How is this helping?

I feel his eyes on me, his gaze heavy. I steal a glance at him, and he's standing still and glaring at me. His face illuminated by the candle is a combination of pain and…something else. Something I'm afraid to identify. Something that makes my chest squeeze.

Adoration.

Desire.

"Not as beautiful as the woman wearing it right now," he says.

I am paralyzed. I'm sinking in his eyes again, forgetting everything else.

Idiot! I break the eye contact. I'm practically swooning, worse than pre-Leonard even. Worse than a teenage girl watching a TV show about vampires and werewolves.

There are small drawers in the bookshelf in front of me, and I open them mechanically. I don't have a candle, and I can't see anything in the darkness.

Turning back to look at him, I see that his gaze falls into a small, square chest he just opened, and he does not move.

"What is it?" I ask.

He dips his hand into the chest and pulls something out, then holds it out to show me. I hurry to him to see better, and there's a small wooden box in his palm with six edges. It's made of dark wood. On two sides there are long, narrow horizontal cuts. I think it's a ventilation system for the crickets.

James and I look at each other—there's triumph, hope, and joy in his eyes. And I know they are also in mine. This is the way for me to go back, to make sure Lisa's all right and not stuck on a pirate ship somewhere. And for him to get the life he wants.

He opens his mouth to say something but snaps it shut as footsteps and a male voice sound behind the door.

The blood drains from my face. My feet feel as if they weigh four hundred pounds each. Like in a nightmare when you want to run but move with the speed of a turtle. Somehow I manage to round the desk to James. "Quick, give me the box," I say.

"Never! Do you think I'm stupid enough to trust a pretty face?"

"Come on." I'm standing right in front of him now. "I'll hide it between my breasts. No one will dare to look there."

He arches one eyebrow, cocks his head, and purses his lips. I can see the "really?" in his eyes. But the door handle is turning. He gives me the box. I stick it between, well technically under, my breasts. I don't really have enough boob material to make it disappear between. The box is a little warm from his touch, and I can't help wishing his fingers were touching me instead of the sharp wooden corners jabbing into my flesh.

Then the door opens, light streaming into the study. The voice is louder now.

James wraps his arms around me and kisses me, and the feel of his soft lips against mine makes me forget everything else.

CHAPTER 8

*ames*

FIRE SEETHES through me as I claim her lips. She's soft and warm and silky. I draw her closer, and her body in my arms is both delicate and strong, and I want her. My pulse is drumming. Swelling with need, I run my hand down her spine. The fullness of her breasts crushing against me makes me drunk, and her sweet scent ignites me like a linstock to a gun.

Lord, I will have her right here, right now. The brave, resourceful, smart, and stubborn seductress.

Someone coughs, and I freeze. "What are you doing in my study?" the governor says.

Damnation. How could I have so completely lost my mind that I forgot someone was about to enter?

Slowly, I stop the kiss and lean back, my eyes still on Samantha. She is panting, her lips red and swollen from the kiss, her eyes dark and shiny, her cheeks flushed. I want to see her like that as I make her mine.

But I must not. Not now, not ever.

I turn to the governor. There is another man standing beside him.

"Forgive me, monsieur, for this display," I say. "In France, we do not mind passion. Your study offered us a refuge."

The governor scans the room, and I realize the small chest I had taken the cricket box from is open. I nonchalantly shift it from view and close it behind my back.

"Matrimonial happiness," the governor says. "Quite delightful."

"The window," Samantha whispers, and sweat covers my back. "The curtain."

She walks towards the window saying, "Excuse me, gentlemen, I need a moment to compose myself."

The governor's companion is following Samantha with his eyes. The lust on his face cuts my gut like sabers. If we did not need to disappear with the box, I would not have forgiven anyone that stare. Not at any woman. And especially not at Samantha. That is how I was raised, and even being a pirate does not change that.

"Governor Richardson," he says, "I quite understand the marquis." He turns to me. "You have a most beautiful wife, sir."

He makes a little bow at me, and I am ready to launch myself at him. Samantha reaches the window and pretends to study the garden, then takes the curtain and draws it a little to cover the shards on the floor and the broken fragments in the frame. I exhale and instruct myself to calm down.

"I do have a beautiful wife," I say through clenched teeth, as Samantha rejoins me. "Now, if you'll forgive us, we will leave you."

I like the sound of her being referred to as my wife, being *mine*, more than I care to admit. My hand on the small of her back, I swallow as sweet flames lick my palm. As I guide her towards the exit, the governor says, "While you are here, Marquis, would it not be a good chance to speak of the sale?"

I stop and turn to him, flashing a polite smile. "Forgive me, monsieur, I do not wish to abandon my wife at the ball. Let us enjoy your hospitality, and I will speak with you of the sale in the days to come."

The governor cocks his head. "Quite so."

I give a small bow and hurry Samantha out of the room.

"Quick, let us be on our way," I say, escorting her through the busy ballroom, out the doors, through the garden, and out the gates.

The governor's house is a twenty-minute walk to the beach where Mr. Killian, the quartermaster and my most trusted man, has hidden a boat for me. Holding hands, Samantha and I run there, down the dusty road that curves through the dark sugarcane fields. The air is fresher here with the sea breeze. My veins sizzle with the joy of victory, just like when I was a boy riding a grown horse for the first time, wind against my face.

The hunt is almost over. Then I can leave this restless life and settle down.

Now that the goal is closer, it does not fill me with the lightness of satisfaction I had wished for. No longer would I roam the seas. No longer would I be captain of my own vessel. I would be someone else. My chest and limbs tighten, and my throat itches.

The road twists into soft, white hills of sand, and the crash of waves breaking against the land reaches my ears.

"You were exquisite, Samantha," I whisper. "I could not have wished for a better fake wife."

She laughs. "We were both great in there. I've never felt such a rush. Never had such an adventure. There's no one I'd rather have lived through it with than with you."

The dunes open up to the beach, which glows gray against

the vast blackness of the ocean and the sky. We walk slower now. I separate from Samantha and walk towards the bushes and a fallen palm tree.

As I get closer to the palm, doubt scratches in my chest like an angry cat. What if the crew succeeded in their mutiny while I was away? What if the boat is not there? My gut is twisting as I separate the bushes with my hands.

I see the boat. Relief lightens my chest.

Now all I need is the cricket box. Then I'm free.

Free from her.

Why does the thought taste bitter in my mouth?

I turn to her. The breeze is playing with the soft curls that have fallen free from her hairdo. She's watching me with a half smile.

"You want the box now, don't you?" she says. "There's your boat." She nods with her chin to the bushes behind me. "All you need is the last piece of the puzzle. And all I need is the jade necklace. We were a great team back there."

My eyes fall to her décolleté, the soft curves of her breasts that the dress is hugging, and my lips burn to brush against them, to lick her skin, to see how smooth they are, how soft.

I swallow. "I do need the last piece of the puzzle." I stretch out my hand. "The cricket box, please."

She raises her chin, the corners of her lips curl up higher.

"Why don't you come and get it?"

Oh, I want to.

But if I do, I do not think I could stop.

"Samantha," I say, and my voice is a warning.

She looks like a fox who just had a whole pen of fresh eggs, her eyes sparkling in the night's darkness.

"It's yours, James," she says, and her voice is a soft feather that brushes against my skin. "Just come and get it."

Something deep in my gut melts. "As you wish, madame."

I hold my hand out and slowly dip two fingers between her breasts. They are warm, and her skin is so smooth my fingers are thawing like ice on a hot stove.

Dear Lord, the need for her whirls and roars in my veins, sweet and mind-altering. The box is under the tips of my fingers, below her breasts. I pinch it and tug. The journey back up brings me more torture because she is so obviously enjoying it. Her head tilts back and her lips part, dark and inviting. Her half-closed eyes are watching me. My fingers slide up, and she licks her bottom lip, then bites it.

I sense she wants to moan but is holding her breath, and I want her to release the moan more than I have wanted anything in my life. My fingers stop midway and stroke the deliciously soft skin of her cleavage.

And there it is. The sweet moan of pleasure escapes her lips as she closes her eyes. The sound sends a burst of fire through my blood, setting me ablaze like dry gunpowder.

I am hers. I cannot take another breath until I kiss her.

Until she is mine.

I remove the box from her breasts and put it in the pocket of my coat, then circle her waist and draw her to me. She gasps as I pull her tight against my chest.

Wrapping her arms around my neck, she kisses me, and I sink into the sea of her scent—sun and coconut and uniquely *her*. Her lips are a soft, luscious heaven; her tongue probes and caresses mine. She is my undoing.

I devour her, claim her. Let her know her mouth is mine.

She is mine.

I dip my tongue into her mouth and meet hers with broad strokes, earning myself another moan, deeper. I caress her body, my hands sliding up and down her back, her shoulders, her arms. She is so pliable yet firm. She answers me with the same heat. My hand slides into the silky softness of her hair.

With my other hand, I dip into her décolleté and release one breast. She gasps, and I break the kiss and look down at it. It is perfect in its milky softness, the nipple dark against her fair skin.

"So perfect," I murmur and take it into my mouth and suck. Her fingers run through my hair and she moans.

"Oh God, James," she says on a sigh.

Her voice…her words are like rum spilled into a flame. I want her. I am burning for her. I am living for her.

Then part of me sobers up.

If I do not stop now, I shall not stop at all. And in that case, I risk everything. After only a few hours with her, my whole being burns for her, needs her. Never have I felt anything like that, not even for Anne.

I cannot allow this.

She might be the end of me.

I stop and withdraw, still leaning over, eyes closed, taking deep breaths. Her hands rest on my shoulders.

"Are you all right?" she breathes out.

I straighten and look at her. She is the goddess of the sea, her face flushed, her lips round and red, one breast seducing me all over again.

I swallow, hoping that the fire in my breeches will calm down.

"I cannot claim you as mine, Samantha," I say. "I cannot."

She throws her hands in the air. "Why not? It's just sex. I want you and you want me. We got your box. Let's celebrate."

I will not tell her the truth. The truth will only reveal too much about how I feel. And I need to forget her. Damnation, it will be difficult as it is. If I have her, I am afraid I shall not be able to let her go.

"You are an unmarried young lady. I cannot compromise you more than I already have."

She shakes her head in disbelief. "What?"

"You are a lady—"

"I am no lady."

"Well, not in title, but you are of a good family. Of a good upbringing. I cannot ruin you."

She gapes. "I am already 'ruined,' James."

CHAPTER 9

amantha

JAMES SHAKES HIS HEAD. "WHAT?"

I'm fuming. I'm tired of his withdrawal. I want him, and I know he wants me. I'm no damsel in distress. I'm a New Yorker, a twenty-first-century woman and a free sexual being. If I want a man, he always wants me back. My breast still hangs out of my dress and embarrassment fuels my anger. I tuck my boob back into the corset.

"I've had enough of you pulling away," I say. "First in the garden and now here… Here's the truth, James. I am from the future and can have sex with whomever I want, whenever I want."

There, I said it. He looks at me as though I've just spoken Mongolian.

"From the future?" he says.

I sigh. "Yes, James. I was born in 1989. I live in New York.

And I was on a vacation in the Caribbean with a friend, Lisa. Who I am desperately telling myself is still back in the future."

His eyebrows knit together, his lips tight. "Do you take me for a fool? You try to seduce me, then say you are from the future? What next, Samantha, do you intend to kill me and take the boat?"

I straighten up. "Of course I'm not going to kill you."

He grabs me by the arm, his face right next to mine, and my stomach knots.

"Leave. Before I am the one doing the killing."

I swallow, my hands and feet drain of all heat. Do the people he raids feel this, too? I'd give him anything he wanted if I were on a ship he was raiding. It's strangely exciting, and the area where he holds my arm burns.

"I'm not leaving." My voice is quieter than I intend it to be. "I'm coming with you. All I need is the jade necklace, then I can travel in time back to the future where I belong. Then I'll leave you be, and you'll never hear of me again."

He lets go of my arm and takes a step back. His jawline hardens, and his head tilts down as he looks at me from under his brows.

"Look," I say, "if I were lying, would I have picked such a ridiculous excuse as time travel? I already had a perfectly believable backstory."

He snorts. "Perfectly believable?"

"Well, more believable. Think about it. My outfit."

"Could be a strange fashion choice."

"The things I know about you."

"Did you not say Cole told you all that?"

"My strange way of speaking."

He shakes his head, but I can tell he is not convinced in his own denial. "What a laughable explanation," he says.

"It's not. That's how I know so much about you. Lisa and I

took a guided tour in a pirate museum, and our guide told us about you and Cole."

With arms crossed over his chest, he looks like he's trying to process everything I've said. When he opens his mouth to say something, I interrupt him. "Do you realize you would have been hanged if you didn't go with someone to the ball tonight? You'd never have gotten this box. You'd eventually go back to Bristol, to your family, and there you'd be hanged for piracy."

His nostrils flare. "This proves nothing. Any pirate is in danger of being hanged."

"True. But I also know you haven't had a successful raid for a couple of months, and your crew is close to staging a mutiny. Cole wouldn't know that—you haven't seen him since the Spanish treasure ship fiasco."

He frowns. "You could have picked that up when you were held in the brig."

Damn it. He's an even a bigger rationalizer than I am. I growl in desperation. I, who could sell water to an ocean.

"I do not have time for your tales," he says. "The governor might have discovered the absence of the box and could be searching for us. I advise you to go and hide while you can."

I take a few steps towards the blackness at the end of the sand. The wind brings the scent of the ocean. I know what to do. "I bet you can't even open that thing," I say.

"What?"

"The box. It's a puzzle." I turn to him, and his eyes narrow. "They aren't easy to open. That's why Cole hid the clue there, because he knew it would keep the secret safe for you."

His face straightens, and he looks at the box in his hands. "You are lying," he growls, turning it this way and that, fiddling with it, trying to find a lock, an opening. Something.

"Damnation!" he roars, then throws it to the sand and runs his hands through his hair. He turns away from me and walks a couple of steps, then kicks the sand.

He looks at me. "Let me guess. You know how to open it."

I raise one eyebrow.

"How?" he says.

"My grandpa collected Japanese puzzle boxes. Some Chinese cricket boxes have the same principle. I've been playing with them since I was a child."

"I can just smash it with a rock and break it open."

Oh damn. Yes, he can.

"What if the clue is damaged?" I say. "What if it's not even on paper?"

James snarls like a wolf. He closes the space between us, takes both my upper arms and shakes me slightly. His eyes practically glow with dark-violet fire. "If you are lying again, I swear to God—"

He breaks off and stares at me.

"What?" I breathe out.

He lets me go without saying another word, turns around and looks for the box on the ground. When he finds it, he hands it to me.

The moment the box is in my hands, he takes out his pistol and points it at me. "One wrong move and you'll find out."

As much as I don't want to admit it, a slight chill slithers through me. There's something about a gun waving in your face to highlight the seriousness of the situation. I doubt he'll shoot me, but fear still washes over me like a cold wave.

I look at the box and turn it in my hands. I'm pretty sure I just need to slide the side panels and it will open. But if I just open the box, he'll ditch me. "I'm not going to help you," I say and hand it back.

His expression is priceless. His mouth practically falls open. "What?"

"I'm not going to help you. Unless you help me."

His lips tighten. "Let me guess—the jade necklace."

"Exactly. The way I see it, either I help you and you get your treasure, minus the necklace, or you have nothing at all."

He lets out a long breath and lowers his pistol. "What would stop me from taking the coordinates and leaving you here?"

I take a step towards him and put a hand on his chest. Even through his vest, I feel his strong heartbeat, and it's racing. My heart begins to accelerate together with his. "Because I want you to give me your word."

"I am a pirate, madame. My word is of no significance."

"Oh, but it is. Your word to Cole is. Your word to your crew is. I want you to give me that same word."

The muscles in his jaw are jumping and his eyes are burning with fury.

"Let it be so," he says.

"So if I help you get the coordinates, you will take me with you and give me the jade necklace?"

"Yes."

"Your word?"

He closes his eyes for a moment. "Yes, woman, my word. Now please, hurry." He looks back at the dunes. "Someone might have spotted us leaving the ball. They may have discovered the broken window."

Despite his earlier threats, I'm excited to spend more time with him, and, frankly, to help him. There's clearly still enough of a gentleman in him not to hurt a woman, especially since he's so worried about ruining me.

I look at the box in detail. I'm not an expert by any means. When I was a small child, the boxes had seemed completely impenetrable to me, and I had been fascinated to watch my granddad move the panels through a series of slides and moves and get each box to open. It always seemed as if he had performed a small miracle. When I was old enough, he taught me how to open them myself.

The precious, bittersweet memories burn my eyes. Well, Grandpa, time for your legacy to help me.

"Hurry, Samantha." James glances at the dunes again.

The box in my hands looks like a thick compact-powder case. On one side, slightly lighter wood repeats the dark form of the box. A carving of a Chinese dragon decorates the other side. I feel the box with the pads of my fingers, scrape the wood with my nails looking for any gaps between the panels. Finally, one of the side panels shifts under my finger. The change is so slight, I almost miss it. I press, and it moves more. A slide, and it comes off completely. With shaking fingers, I hand the free panel to James.

I probe the panel next to it. There's the slightest movement, and I push to slide it off. Now two sides of the hexagon are off. It's dark, so I cannot see much. James takes the box from my hands and peers inside, then turns it over and shakes.

"Empty," he says, his voice lifeless.

"Wait. We haven't opened it completely. Let me see."

I take the box back and try to slide the third side, but it doesn't move. My fingers chill, all the excitement vanished. I press harder on the side, but still nothing. I explore the interior but find nothing.

"Did someone open it before us?" I ask. "Why is it empty?"

James spits a curse that makes even me blush.

I continue to feel and press, and then it hits me. The hexagon on the cover. There's a slight color difference in the wood bordering where the two slides once were. I press on the cover and it slides, opening the box, but anger replaces my moment of hope. It really is empty.

Completely, utterly empty.

"No," I whisper. "It can't be."

Is that it? Am I stuck in the eighteenth century forever? Is my life here now? With that thought, the very air presses in on me from all sides. I can't stay here. My life is in New York. What about my lovely apartment? What about my promotion?

"Maybe there's a double bottom," he says. "Let me see."

He takes the box and presses on the bottom. "Something moved."

I hold my breath as he fiddles with it more. Please, please let there be a double bottom.

After long, excruciating moments that stretch out like an eternity, the hexagon bottom is in his hand. The box falls on the ground, and he's holding a folded piece of paper.

My mouth goes dry. I lean against him, trying to see what is in there, and he shifts right next to me, his side touching mine. "What does it say?"

A current runs between us sending liquid bliss through my veins. Our eyes lock for a moment, and desire sparks between us. He unfolds the paper and looks at it for a long time. "What is it?" I ask. He turns it to me, and I see two rows of numbers, the signs of degrees and minutes.

"The coordinates," James says, and his face seems to shine.

The thumping of my heart is so loud and fast it's about to jump out of my chest. One step closer to home. "Shall we go there? They might chase us, right?"

But I'm not ready to go. Not from here, not from James's powerful proximity. His closeness, his scent ensnares me. If only I reach out a little bit, I can kiss him again.

As if he's reading my thoughts, he turns to me and claims my mouth.

CHAPTER 10

amantha

H*e's not just kissing* me, he's devouring me. His lips are a tornado and I'm the house on the prairie, torn apart in the most delicious way.

Wrapping his arms around me, he pulls me tighter to him, heat sizzles through my veins and my body melts against him like wax in the Caribbean sunlight. He runs his lips and his tongue down my neck, making every cell of my skin burn.

Arching into the sweet prison of his arms, I run my fingers through his silky hair and sink into his scent—clean linen, sandalwood, and sun.

From the direction of the dunes, a twig snaps and James breaks the kiss and tugs me after him. Tucked behind the bushes with the hidden boat, under the palm trees where shadows reign, we crouch and listen. But the beach remains silent, only waves whisper and the breeze rustles through the leaves. Risk electrifies my whole body. With his arms around me, James turns me to look at him.

"If anyone comes, I will protect you, Samantha," he says, then glances at my lips. "You are safe with me. But maybe not from me."

He's looking at my mouth as if he's in agony and it's the painkiller. He leans to my lips, and I whisper, "What about the whole ruining me thing?"

"I was wrong," he says, and the breeze kisses my cheeks with the scent of the sea and mango. "It is me who will be ruined if I do not have you."

He kisses me again, letting me sink deeper into the warm sea of desire. His hands unlace my dress and tug the bodice down to my waist. When the warm night air touches my skin, it breathes again. James releases the lace of the corset, and when he throws it aside, I take a lungful of air sending my head spinning. When he caresses my skin under the shift, I fly high. He strokes me, massages my back, my breasts, my waist. Prickling, sizzling, expanding after hours of being trapped in the corset, my skin and muscles sing under his touch.

I run my hands over his broad shoulders, his muscles hard under the shirt. Off comes his jacket, then his waistcoat, and my fingers crawl over the linen of his shirt covering his firm stomach.

My breath rushes out of me as I pull away to look at him. "I need to see you."

His smile is both wicked and tight, and he spreads his arms in an invitation. "Please do, madame."

I take the edges of his shirt and pull them up, tugging it over his head. What I see under it fills my mouth with saliva. All muscle, his body is lean and perfect. His pecs make my palms ache to brush them, his six-pack looks carved of stone. A long, thin silver scar runs across the left side of his chest down to his solar plexus. There's also a round pale-pink one on his side that must be newer. Though his face and hands are tanned from years on the open sea, the skin under his shirt is fair, his chest lightly covered in soft blond hair. His shoulders and biceps are like smooth, round rocks.

"Wow," escapes my lips, my mouth as dry as cardboard.

He chuckles and pulls me to him. "Now it is my turn to free you of your clothes."

And that he does. He pulls me up and tugs down my dress gathered at my waist together with the panniers. When I stand before him in my shift, he pulls it up and over my head, leaving me only in the stockings, my panties, and the shoes. I'm vulnerable under his burning gaze and stop the urge to cover myself.

Why do I feel as though it's the first time?

First time on the beach. First time since Leonard what I want is more than just sex. This is like making love.

Making love is something Lisa would say. I do not make love. I have sex, like a man, leaving emotions aside. At least that's what I'm telling myself, waiting until I fully believe it. I must be careful with James, because this feels too good.

But even given all this, I can't stop.

His gaze snakes up and down my body and leaves warm traces behind.

"Lord Almighty," he says. "I have seen no one as beautiful."

The words start a low burning fire in me, my blood turning into simmering caramel.

"What are these small pants you are wearing?"

"Underwear. What, women in your time don't have those?"

He chuckles. "Are you still insisting that you traveled in time? I'll play along. Not such small underwear. And not the women of high social rank."

He pulls me to him, and we sink onto the blanket of our combined clothes. He claims my lips again, turning the simmering into a full-blown boil. His fingers trace down and sparks prickle between my skin and his hands. And when he finds my breast, he takes the nipple between his thumb and his fingers and massages it. Then he sucks, licks, teases it, and I dissolve in him.

Until he goes to the second breast and repeats the same there, and my knees melt like butter on a stove.

I run my hands over his hard body, enjoying his smooth skin, the crispiness of his hair on his chest and stomach. He's moving down and kissing my stomach, going lower and lower. Until his face is level with the juncture of my thighs. He pulls my panties off, then freezes and looks up at me.

"Where is your hair?"

Right. I went for a Brazilian wax in preparation for the vacation. I chuckle and my cheeks burn. "Do you like it?"

He brushes his fingers along my sensitive cleft. "So smooth," he whispers against my skin. I arch my back as his touch sends a wave of what feels like liquid velvet through me.

A moan escapes my throat. He brushes his fingers against me there, over and over, his fingers featherlight, teasing, and turning me on so much that perspiration covers my skin.

His hand spreads my legs and they fall open for him. He is still kneading my breast with one hand while the fingers of the other parts me. "All mine," he says. My insides clench, and I almost come from his words alone.

He kisses me then, right there. His tongue is going in circles around my clitoris, spilling pleasure like warm wine down my limbs. He is teasing and pressing and sucking, and I'm mindless with bliss. I'm somewhere on another planet, in another world, in between centuries. My muscles clench around him with a deep ache. I'm writhing.

But this is not enough. I want him.

"I don't want to come yet," I breathe out. "I want you inside of me."

He straightens and rises on his knees, then removes his breeches. His erection springs free.

"Oh," I whisper.

He lowers, supporting himself on straight arms and our eyes lock. The man I see is bare and vulnerable. I choke a bit from the awe and lust glimmering in his eyes and the feelings reverberate within me. As if I'm a long-awaited prize. As if I'm something divine and he worships me.

No one has ever looked at me like that. Not even the man I thought was the love of my life.

James is right between my thighs, and they are smoldering. I'm all wet and hot down there, sleek with desire.

"How do you want me?" he says.

My hands on his hips, I'm just about to tug him toward me when he freezes and looks up. In the heat of the moment I forgot everything else, but, thankfully, James did not.

Because as I freeze and follow his gaze, the sound of hooves comes from behind the dunes.

CHAPTER 11

ames

THE THUMPING of hooves is still quiet, so they must be far away. My whole body is like hot molasses as I leave my moon goddess and dress.

My gut knots and my chest is heavy as I force myself not to pull Samantha back into my arms. The clothes feel wrong on my skin. I am still aroused, although the breeze is helping me to cool off. Whether the intruders are the governor's men or someone else, they do not want anything good with us.

"We should have left earlier," I say through gritted teeth.

Samantha dresses, too, cursing the amount of clothes. She puts on the shift and the dress and leaves the rest on the ground.

"We must take the boat into the sea," I say.

"Won't they notice?"

"They are still far enough away. We must make haste."

She nods and we go through the bushes to the boat. I right the overturned boat and we drag it over the sand towards the water's edge, which is about twenty yards away. The thudding of hooves is closer now. They must be right behind the last of the dunes. Samantha and I are only halfway across the beach.

They will be upon us any moment.

"Hide behind the bushes," I command.

She straightens and watches me.

"There's no time to waste. Quickly, behind the bushes. Do as I say."

She nods and rushes there, then disappears. I take my pistol and sink behind the boat, then peer at the beach. I resolve to use my cunning. They will likely come to the boat to inspect it, and my plan is to shoot one with my pistol and fight the other one with my knife.

Two riders appear from behind the dunes. They slow and look around the beach. They get down off their horses and walk towards the boat. This is my chance.

Although it is night, there is enough moonlight to allow me to see them quite clearly. I move the hammer to full cock and aim. When my target is clear, I pull the trigger and the flintlock explodes with a loud *bang* and an explosion of sparks and smoke. The man screams, is kicked back and falls.

The other one darts for the bushes where Samantha hides.

Ice needles pierce my entire body as I run there, too. I have no time to reload the pistol, and I remove the knife from my boot. The shadow of the man darts into the bushes, and I follow.

I hear a *thump* and Samantha screams, her voice shrill. I speed up, and there she is.

In the arms of a redcoat, his pistol at her temple.

Fear grasps me, tightens my throat, slashes my gut like a saber.

I lock eyes with her. She's terrified but not showing it. I see a prospect before me, but I need her to trust me, and she must do it without me telling her to.

"Kill her," I say. "She is of no consequence to me."

Her eyes widen. The redcoat frowns and shoots a quick glance at her. "What?"

"She's just another wench."

Samantha frowns and stares at me, then her eyebrows rise in realization. She understands the game I'm playing. Smart, intuitive woman. The trust she puts in me makes my lungs tighten.

"Yes, sir," she says. "Please, save me. He kidnapped me and seduced me. I'm so glad you came and freed me from this dirty pirate."

Her words sting a little. *Dirty pirate?* Her eyes soften, as though she is apologizing.

The redcoat studies her, confusion mixed with doubt on his face. Then he lets her go and pushes her behind him, pointing the barrel right in my face. I sigh with relief—Samantha is safe for now. I hold my hands up.

"Madame, stay behind me," he says. "What is your name, sir?"

I chuckle as I see Samantha taking a large piece of driftwood in both her hands behind him. "James 'Prince' Barrow," I say, and observe with delight how his face pales.

At that moment, Samantha hits the back of his head with the driftwood, and I launch at him with my knife. He falls to the ground, and I put my knife to his throat. But he has lost consciousness and there's no need to kill him. I stand up and look at Samantha.

"Are you all right?" I ask as Samantha flies into my arms. I pull her tighter to me, pressing my lips to the top of her head and inhaling her heavenly scent.

She's shaking slightly in my arms, and I'm surprised. She looked so brave just a moment ago. I rub her arm up and down to warm her.

"We need to tie him up," she says, and her breath heats me through my shirt.

She looks up at me with eyes as dark as the night sea. I sink into them, forgetting the danger, the unconscious man lying at my feet, and the second one a few feet away. I lower my head and kiss her, the need for her closeness roaring in me like wildfire.

I have barely begun feasting on her lips when the redcoat moans. With regret, I interrupt the kiss.

"You are correct, Samantha, we need to tie him up. Would you be so kind to tear off some of your shift, please?"

The man is waking up, and I hold him while she lifts the skirt of her dress and tears off three long pieces of cloth. I gag his mouth, then drag him to the palm tree and tie his hands behind him, and then him to the tree. I take his pistol and his cutlass and go check the other man. He has a wound at his hip and is unconscious but still alive. I relieve him of his weapons, as well.

Then I return to my fair lady *time traveler*. My conscious mind refuses to believe her words, but in my heart, I feel their truth. The trust, the bond between us is strong. And it is terrifying.

"We must make haste now, Samantha. Let us take the boat to the water. I need to determine the course with the coordinates on land, but let us be near the boat so we are ready to go at once in case more men come."

She nods. "Sounds like a plan. Come on."

We continue to drag the boat towards the sea, and once it's right at the water's edge, I remove the maritime map and the instruments to measure the course. I put them on the sand, and as I'm doing my calculations and measuring the course, I realize I'm feeling something I haven't felt for a long time—a sense of connection. The feeling of working as a well-coordinated crew.

It's something I've always envisaged a relationship with a woman could be.

But a dull ache pierces me as I shove the feelings deep down. I cannot allow them. I must not fall under the spell of a woman like her. She has no intention of staying with me. She is going to travel back to her time once we find the necklace.

And I am going to stay here and try to forget her.

CHAPTER 12

amantha

JAMES STANDS next to me on the quarterdeck, the spyglass pressed to one eye. He points at the land on the horizon. "That's where we are heading. Not much longer now."

My stomach sinks. The clock is ticking. Not much longer till I'm gone.

The ship rocks on heavy waves as we sail at full speed. After we returned to the ship from New Providence Island, the wind had picked up and the waves had begun rolling like small hills. I managed to sleep for a few hours while James was busy with his captain's duties. I wanted to stay awake while I waited for him in his cabin, but I drifted off and just woke up half an hour ago. He was sitting in the armchair watching me in the gray light of the morning. My lips curled in a smile. Seeing him first thing after I opened my eyes made me feel as though I might float up into the sky like a helium balloon.

After a short breakfast, I had come out onto the quarterdeck to see was going on. The sky is full of small dark clouds. The gale fills the sails and the huge waves make my stomach drop and my head spin.

New Providence Island, with its soldiers, is long gone, but the hard knot in my gut that had formed after the redcoats found us, only tightens. There seems to be no end to the adventures as the sea tries it's damnedest to capsize the ship. I inhale, trying to relax, drinking in the wet, salty air of the Atlantic.

I look at James to calm down. His hair is escaping its short seaman's braid and frames his gorgeous face. His white shirt is open at his chest, and the sight of his broad shoulders and strong chest beneath makes my throat thicken. My God, he's so handsome my chest tightens and squeezes with a sweet ache. He looks at me, his eyes hold me, and his gaze warms my skin.

Part of me still doesn't believe he's real and that he wants me. Even if I pretend to be this woman who can have it all, there's still the young romantic inside of me who wants unconditional love.

And James has reached out for that small part of me and is holding its hand.

And I'm terrified.

"What happens once we find the treasure?" I ask.

A wave hits the ship and the floor sinks under my feet, and I grip the bulwarks. He frowns and an expression of vulnerability flashes across his face. "What would you like to happen?"

"I want to go back to my time." But I also don't want to leave you. "What would *you* like to happen?"

His gaze darkens. "I would like you to stay longer. I want to continue what we started on the beach. I want to make you scream my name as I give you your release and as you give me mine."

The world freezes and my cheeks burn. My fingers grip the

wooden side of the ship as I struggle to get enough air into my lungs. My mouth waters and I swallow hard.

"Would you like that?" he asks, his face showing the wicked, wolfish grin of a predator.

I gulp down a yes. I want to allow myself this last treat before I leave. Before I never see him again. But I can't. What happened between us on the island must be enough. "I won't stay, James. I want us to be crystal clear about that."

He frowns, then his face relaxes, but there's still tension around his mouth. "I will not stop you, Samantha."

Even though this is what I want to hear, my throat hurts and my eyes prickle as his words hit me. A big wave slams us again, and the ship crests and then plummets down the back of it. I grab the bulwarks with both hands, feeling woozy.

"Are you all right, Samantha?" James asks.

"How are you not even grabbing onto anything in this storm?"

"This is not a storm. Are you worried?"

"Aren't you?"

He crosses his arms, seducing me with the sight of his muscled forearms. "Fine. Let me distract you. When you get back, does a fiancé or a man who courts you wait for you? Is that why you wish to go back so much?"

"No. I don't want a fiancé or a husband or anyone courting me."

In fact, often I'm the one doing the "courting."

"Oh?" he says. "Do you not wish to get married, then?"

"No. I don't want to fall in love. Not again."

"Did someone break your heart?"

Now, the storm forgotten, I know I'm going to bleed if I tell him. I don't want to remember Leonard, but I feel like I want to share my story with James. He seems to care enough to ask. And yet, opening up is like tearing my heart out with my own hands.

"Yeah," I say.

He narrows his eyes at me. "It seems we have both had our share of heartbreak."

He quiets, as if expecting me to take the bait and talk about it. "Let's drop it, please," I say.

"If you intend to go back soon, I shall be gone from your life forever. You might as well confide in me."

He's right, of course, although I don't want him to be gone from my life forever. But this adventure will come to its end. It must. Confiding in him is actually tempting, and I know it's probably been less than twelve hours since I met him, but it feels like I've known him so much longer. Especially after everything we've gone through together. We dealt with those soldiers like a team. I trust him more than I have any other man in my life since Leonard.

Maybe even more than Leonard.

And that's terrifying. Like, soul-shattering, ground-sinking, heart-tearing terrifying. Because if Leonard had broken my heart like that, what would falling for James do?

Behind James, the land is ever closer. We'll be there soon, and the need to tell him grows in me, itches me like a wound under a cast. Can I really tell him? Let him know that the mask of this confident woman who pretends to have it all is just a lie? That beneath it I'm weak and terrified of another heartbreak. That all I'm doing by pushing men away is protecting myself, hurting them before they can hurt me.

I know I'm a coward because I won't give him a chance. Because even if in some crazy alternate universe we could be together, I would probably screw up the relationship, terrified he'd know the real me.

But I won't stay, and in a few hours I'll never see him again.

And I let go. "I was twenty-one when I met him. I'd never been in a serious relationship before. I was a bit like my friend Lisa, naive, always looking for that one true love."

Saying that makes my throat clench, and I choke a bit and pause. James holds me in his gaze with such intensity, as though his life depends on what I say next. The ship drops again and shakes a little, and my eyes shoot to the sea.

"Talk," he commands. "Forget about the waves."

"And I thought I had met my true love in Leonard. I was studying at Columbia University then."

James raises his eyebrows. "Women are allowed to attend university in the future?"

I chuckle, his comment lightening me up a bit. "Yeah. We also go to work and run businesses and buy our own houses."

He smiles. "A beneficial future for the world, smart and strong women in command. I always envisioned having one by my side—before she betrayed me."

My face heats up.

"What happened next with that man—Leonard?" He scowls as he says the name.

"He..." I start to pick my fingernails, a bad habit I haven't done since Leonard. "He was a professor of economics and fifteen years older than me. Our relationship was against the university policy, so we kept it a secret. I'd always thought that true love changes you. Well, he did. At twenty-one, I was still so naive about the world, about life, about everything. But with him, I grew up, started to believe in myself and feel more like a woman."

A gust of wind steals the words from my mouth and chokes me, and James covers my hand with his. "Go on," he says.

Our eyes lock. "While we were together, all I could think about was him. I started dressing differently, more appropriate for a professor's wife. Honestly, I went a bit crazy. If he didn't answer my calls, I went looking for him. I practically stalked him. I craved him, as if I were no one without him. He started pulling away and soon just stopped responding to my calls, my texts, my emails. When I saw him, he addressed me as Miss Gilbert, as though I were a stranger."

The ship lurches, but my stomach is already sour from the memories. The winds ease a bit and the sky begins to clear. A cloud drifts by, freeing the way for the sun. The rays kiss the side of James's face, making his left eye seem almost blue. His hair glows golden. He's like an angel with a fierce expression. Tears burn my eyes, but I refuse to let them fall. He is giving me strength.

"I felt like a used tissue," I continue. "It was close to graduation, so I dived into working on my thesis. Not long after he dumped me, I found out that I wasn't the first nor the last one he used."

James takes my hands in his and they are big and hot. They reassure me and make me feel steady.

"I should have filed a complaint against him or something. But I was about to graduate, and I just wanted to put it all behind me and start fresh. That was when I decided I wouldn't let a man hurt me like that ever again. I'd become someone new. I'd be the one in control. I haven't had a serious relationship since."

He pulls my hands to his mouth and kisses them, closing his eyes as if the touch of my hands against his lips gives him physical pleasure. His warm lips pressed against my skin spread warmth through my arms like mulled wine on a chilly winter's day.

"I'd kill him if I ever met him," James says, and I smile. Here's a man who wants to protect me from the heartbreaks of the past.

"Thankfully, your meeting will never happen," I say and chuckle, then I freeze. "Oh my God. This is the first time I've smiled or laughed about that situation." I meet his eyes. "Thank you."

"If I manage to make you smile like this again, I will consider my life worth living."

Something floats between us, some sort of magic.

Time stops.

The ship freezes.

The wind stills.

And I wonder if I gave up on love too soon.

CHAPTER 13

ames

"Why is it that you don't have a woman in your life?" Samantha says, her voice soft as silk. "No one to go to a ball with you."

She has just poured her heart to me, and I am furious at the man who hurt her so much, but lightness and softness fill my chest because she trusted me with her heart. The invisible strings between us are back, and they pull us closer together.

And I want to tell her.

I need to tell her.

"Anne," I say, my voice coming out as a rasp. The ship jerks a little from the wind as though shuddering along with me at the name. "You heard about her."

"I did. But what happened? What did she do?"

"I thought I was in love with her." I look at the horizon, remembering. "I thought she needed protection. She seduced me. Not that I resisted or was a young, innocent boy. I wanted her. She was—"

Samantha's eyes blur with pain a little.

"I am sorry," I say. "You do not want to hear that."

"No, I do. Please. I just hate her for doing this to you."

I smile. Her support warms me.

"We had an affair. She was smart, beautiful, and she had the will and ambition of a man. I had thought, at first, she was a noble lady, but it was only an act. She acted a lot, liked the attention. Later, I found out that she had her own pirate ship, which only spurred my infatuation with her. I imagined us together, sailing the seas, looking for adventure. Then after a few years, once we had enough of chasing treasures and risking our lives, I thought we would settle somewhere where no one would know who we were. Imagined us opening a proper business together. Starting a family. A family for whom I could provide safety and prosperity."

I shake my head and look at my boots. Samantha covers my hand with hers, and I squeeze it back.

"I was a fool." I meet her dark, endless eyes, which shine with compassion and understanding. Our stories are similar.

"We planned a coup, a raid on a Spanish treasure ship—Anne, Cole, and I—and agreed to share the treasure. Then I would retire with Anne, and Cole would run away to the East. It was a man-o'-war, so we needed all three of us. But in the midst of it all, boarding the ship, battling the Spanish, the English Navy appeared. Cole managed to run away. Anne did not want me to leave, and while we were on board the Spanish ship, she began fighting me to stop me."

I rub my hand against the scar on my torso.

"She told me that giving me and Cole to the British was her and her husband's—the famous pirate Samuel van Huisen—way to get pardoned. It turned out, she wanted to settle down, too. Just not with me."

A bitter, tight knot forms in my throat.

"I managed to run away, thanks to my crew. She was hanged by the British because she failed to deliver what she had promised. I doubt they would have upheld their end of the bargain even if she had gotten me and Cole captured."

Samantha looks me in the eye, and there's such softness and something resembling love in them that I want to take her into my arms and kiss her and never let her go. Telling all this to her feels liberating, and I know we share a wound that is similar.

But just as I am about to pull her into my arms, a sailor appears next to us. "Cap'n, we shall be there soon."

I glance at the land, and it's already in close proximity, probably a boat ride away. Damnation. I am both glad to see the island and hate the sight of it.

Because it means that my path with Samantha is about to end.

The thought is as sobering as a bucket of ice water thrown over me. Yes, we share a common pain, but so what? I understand her reason for being like this. But it does not change the facts. I am falling in love with her, but she does not want a husband. And I do not want to grow old alone.

"Prepare the anchors," I say to the sailor.

When Samantha looks at me again, the magic is gone and her eyes are worried, searching my face.

"It seems that our journey is about to end," I say. "It is good that you and I belong to different worlds. You do not wish to marry. Whereas, after we find the treasure and my pirate days are behind me, there is nothing I want more than a wife and a happy stock of children."

I turn and walk away to command the ship. And even though my mind understands the truth of these words, my chest hurts, and the pain is worse than it was with Anne.

CHAPTER 14

ames

When Samantha and I arrive at the island, the sight takes my breath away. White sand is brilliant against the green jungle and the single low, dark mountain in the middle with a flat top. Although it emits no smoke or ashes, the whole island looks like a broad, sunken volcano. The top is where we must go.

I pull the boat onto the small beach that lies protected between two giant boulders the size of buildings. The beach and the boulders form a horseshoe of sorts. A few palm trees sway in the wind, their fronds waving like horses' manes. The island must measure only a few square miles and is likely uninhabitable. Too small for a proper settlement, and too far away from the nearest populated land. It is no mystery why Cole hid the treasure here.

Samantha stands next to me, and her delicious scent tickles my nostrils and warms my blood. Sparks fly from the touch of our hands. Our eyes lock, and I sink in the depth of hers. I tense and step away from her so as not to dwell on my feelings. I must not indulge.

"The mountain is where we shall go," I say to Samantha as I study Cole's map of the island with instructions on how to find the chest.

Samantha looks dubiously at the long skirt of her dress. "Hmm." She stretches a hand towards the cutlass tucked at my belt. "May I have your sword?"

My brows shoot up. "My cutlass?"

She rolls her eyes. "I'm not going to attack you, James. I just want to cut these skirts. I can't imagine hiking in these."

I hide a smile. She is going to destroy the last memento I have left of Anne. Surprisingly, no pain comes when I think of the woman who betrayed me, no regrets over having nothing left that would remind me of her.

"Allow me," I say. I take her skirts, pinch them between my thumb and index finger, and stretch them out. I pierce them with my cutlass, then tear off the lower part and throw it away. The skirt now ends just above her knees. At the sight of her beautiful bare legs, I cannot resist tracing the smooth skin of her inner thigh with my fingers. I gulp, barely able to restrain myself from lifting her into my arms and having her wrap her delicious legs around my waist. I meet her gaze.

"Is that better?" I ask, my mouth as dry as the sand beneath our feet.

"Much better." She studies me, her eyes like molten starlight. They burn me, they call to me, they challenge. Remembered images of her naked body on the beach in the moonlight flood my psyche, the sweet scent of her sex awakening a desire to howl like a wolf, the echo of her moans of pleasure singing in my ears like the calls of sirens.

"Do you like it?" she asks.

"More than you can ever know," I say hoarsely. "But I cannot submit to my desires. First, I must find the treasure. Our delay back on New Providence Island barely allowed us to escape. Who knows who or what might be up there. The island looks empty, but I do not know that for sure."

Samantha glances at the mountain. "Let's go then."

We head into the bushes and undergrowth, between the rocks and the palm trees. I lead the way, my cutlass ready, though there are no beasts other than birds and buzzing insects, and no signs of men. Glancing back at Samantha from time to time, I make sure she is all right. She looks as fierce and confident as though she has been hiking tropical mountains her whole life. The only thing she is missing is a pistol or a knife.

Soon, the climb becomes steeper and rockier. I step more and more carefully, sometimes moving the rocks with my foot to make sure it is safe to step on them. When we are about halfway to the top, I hear something that makes me freeze and listen. Samantha stops next to me. There's a whisper in the air, like waves hitting the shore but more constant.

"Is that—" she says, and I finish her question.

"—a waterfall."

We are on the right track. Cole marked the waterfall on the map of the island. We speed up and then edge around a large piece of rock that looks more like a piece of frozen lava wall, and there it is, a waterfall. It cascades from the very top of the mountain, where the rocks split, and becomes a thin ribbon of water. The stream is white against the dark surface of the slope and falls into a small pool that looks like a giant, uneven chalice above a small strip of land. Then it falls freely from the other side of the chalice, which hangs above the path. It creates an arch of sorts, then disappears in the greenery below the slope.

"Wow," Samantha whispers and lays her hand on my forearm. "This is amazing."

As beautiful as nature is before us, it is not the sight of the waterfall that holds my breath and makes my throat clench. It is the sight of Samantha's awed face and the pleasant buzzing of my skin where her hand touches me.

She leaves my side and walks towards the falling water, puts her cupped hands into the stream, drinks from it, and closes her eyes in bliss. Then she lets out a small laugh. Taking more water into her palms, she splashes her face with it. Water slips down her neck to her décolleté and wets the edge of her bodice.

"God, this water is so pure. It tastes sweet. Come on, James. Try some."

I stand next to her, and she brings me the water in her cupped palms. I drink, my eyes on her. I lick her palm and she giggles. When the water is gone, I kiss her palms and she stops breathing.

"It is not the water that is sweet," I murmur against her skin. "It is you."

I straighten and gaze into her eyes. Her neck and her chest glisten with droplets as if covered with morning dew, and even though I have just had some water, my mouth goes dry from the thirst for her. I want to lick her skin dry and make her wet in other places.

But I know if I start, I shall not be able to stop. And I must. She must go, and I must let her. She is not the woman for me. No matter how much I desire her, I can never trust another woman as strong as her. And even if I did, she would never stay.

"Come," I say. "Let us be on our way."

Her eyes cloud with a hurt that slashes my heart like a knife, but I turn and walk through the waterfall and up the mountain slope. In an hour or so, we reach the very top, which looks like a giant dune. I climb over it and stop, taking it all in. Samantha stands next to me. It seems as if we are on top of the world, the island beneath our feet like a dark-green hill in the middle of the blue vastness of the ocean. I see my ship anchored not far away.

On the other side of the rocks is a crater with a small blue lake not wider than a hundred feet. It feeds the waterfall we passed. The lake is as flat as a mirror, and looks as if it's a window into a different sky with white clouds flowing by. The slopes of the crater are mostly dark volcanic sand with occasional bushes and grass.

Cole hid the chest in the lake. According to the map, the water is not deep where the chest is, and it is buried in the space between two rocks that protrude into the lake.

I help Samantha down a steep rise. After a short walk, we stand by the lake. The water is crystal clear here and between the two sharp rocks that jut above the surface of the lake like balconies without railings. Under the water, there's a small rocky slope, a collection of stones and rocks.

My gut twists and my heart races. I jump into the water, which splashes around me and onto the shore. It is now around noon and the cold water is welcome in the heat. One after another, I remove the rocks and there it is, the chest.

I stand still and look at it for a minute, my arms refusing to move. Samantha's gaze on my skin is heavy.

"It's there," she says, her voice almost a whisper. "You found it."

I stare at the chest, which looks as if it is swaying under the moving water, and I'm torn inside with the relief and victory of finally finding it and the pain of knowing I shall soon lose her.

"Do you need help pulling it up?" she asks.

"No."

"Then what are you waiting for?"

I meet her eyes, finally. "Once it is on shore there will be nothing to stop you from leaving me forever."

She lowers her gaze and says nothing.

At least she has the decency not to pretend she will change her mind.

There is nothing to say anymore, and I sink into the water and lift the chest. It floats up, supported by the water. But as I bring it towards the shore, it gets heavier. I pull it up onto the ground and jump up, too, my cold, wet clothes clinging to my body. I crouch in front of the chest and open it. Gold and jewels glisten in the sun, still wet.

And in the middle of them, the jade pendant.

This is it. She will go. Without looking at Samantha, I take the necklace in my hands to give it to her, but she gently clasps my hands in hers.

With a dull ache that tears apart my gut and my chest, I look up at her. She crawls closer to me and sits on my lap. Her arms wrap around my neck, and she says, "I don't want to go just yet. There's still one thing I need to do."

Despite the chill of my wet clothes, heat rushes through me. "What is that?"

"Let me show you."

CHAPTER 15

*S*amantha

MY LIPS melt against James's mouth, which meets them, soft and silky and hot. I have butterflies in every cell of my body. The violent beating of my pulse rages in my ears.

The jade necklace lying among the golden coins burns the edge of my vision. The moment that I lose James forever lies at my fingertips. The thought opens a gaping, black, sucking hole in the pit of my stomach.

Not yet. I can't lose him. The need to feel him close, physically and emotionally, for the last time, burns me, urges me.

Body to body, skin to skin, soul to soul—I want him. I need him.

And no tomorrow.

James engulfs me in his strong arms. As he presses me against him, his wet clothes soak my dress, but I don't care. He smells like wet linen and the musk of a man. Combined with the beauty and the magic of the crater lake, shielded from the wind and warmed by the Caribbean sun, he makes me feel like I'm floating.

I undo the buttons of his shirt and pull it off him, the velvet of his damp, cool skin warms my fingertips. His shirt comes off and I trace my fingers down his hard chest, along the line of his scar, down his ripped stomach, his hair soft against my palms. As I do so, I feel his breath accelerate and deepen at the same time.

The slickness of his tongue sets me on fire as he licks and caresses mine, as he sucks and nips at my lips with just the right amount of pressure that makes my insides burn and squeeze and dampen.

He undoes the laces of my jade dress, then breaks contact and undresses me. I drink in every last detail of him: his dark-violet eyes, the gold of his hair, the straight line of his jaw, his full lips, the stubble that ranges from wheat to amber. As he pulls down the bodice of my dress, he kisses the skin that he reveals, spreading bliss through my nervous system like the most exquisite champagne.

My head rolls back, and I arch into his mouth when he gets to my breasts. As he teases them, massages them, sucks on my nipples, plays over them with his tongue, I hear a moan escape my throat. James lays me on the warm, smooth rock that heats my back like the stones in a spa. He pulls down my skirts and removes my shoes, and I lie in front of him, naked and open and burning.

I want him to cover me with his body, but he freezes while kneeling before me. His eyes travel my body from the toes up, and it's like another way of making love. His gaze doesn't make me feel shy or embarrassed. I glow, I open up, and I soften.

"Look at you," he groans. "So beautiful. There's a chest of pearls, jewels, gold and gemstones, and yet they all pale next to you."

My cheeks heat, and I stretch my arms to him. "Come here."

But he doesn't. He glances at the chest and a wicked smile spreads across his lips. "What I want to do, is to see exactly how they pale next to you. I intend a direct comparison."

I bite my lip and hold my breath as I watch him lean to the chest and take something out. A large golden coin that still glistens with water in the sunlight.

"Absorb the sensation, Samantha." He puts the coin on my belly.

I gasp from the sharp bite of cold against the warmth of my skin, and everything squeezes inside of me. I arch my back and let the coolness spread, and strangely, it heats me up. But I tense and a dull but pleasant ache spills across my nerves.

James studies me. "You are still more beautiful than the gold. Let us try something else, a gemstone."

He rummages in the chest again and removes a gold necklace with a large ruby pendant in the form of a teardrop. It catches the sunlight and glows. He leans over me on one straight arm, and I take a quick breath as a cool drop of water lands between my breasts.

"Absorb the sensation," he murmurs.

The necklace lands on my breast, and instantly my nipples harden. I suck in the air as the tightness of the tissue on my breasts makes my nerve endings sing and vibrate. James traces the ruby around my nipple and all my being stiffens. I struggle to keep still.

"Take it in," he says.

And, as though his words are a spell, I do. I breathe out, and instead of fighting the coldness that feels alien, unwelcome, I inhale and take it in, and a whole new world of sensations explodes within me. Heat and tingling and the rush of liquid sunlight. James moves to the other breast, circling the nipple with the smoothness of the gold and ruby. The necklace caresses my skin, continuing the sweet torture, taking me higher than I've ever been before.

"That is right, my sweet," he whispers, against my breast, and his warm breath scorches me like hot lava. "And yet you still win against even these jewels."

"Then plunder me, my pirate," I say.

He smirks and puts the jewels away, then slowly removes his belt, revealing the lower part of his ripped stomach. He pushes down his trousers, inching them over his hips, down strong thighs covered in pale hair. He stands up and kicks the trousers aside, and his erection makes my mouth water. He's so hard, and so big, and when he sinks to his knees, I take his cock in my hand. It's velvety, and I'm thinking I might be going insane from lust. I make a fist around him and caress him, stroke him up and down, and he tilts his head back and moans.

Wow. I can't believe I'm making this man so hard he's unable to control his reaction to me.

I seriously can't take it anymore. I need my release. Now. "Hard and fast," I plead, trying to sink his cock into me. But James isn't moving.

"Oh no, madame," he says. "Hard and fast is for a quick release. You think you want it. But you want slow. Slow and tender and gentle."

I'm alert, my muscles tense to sit up. Slow and tender and gentle is for people in love. I'm not in love with him. I can't be. I just met him and if all goes well, very soon I'll never see him again. Ever since Leonard, that's how sex has been. Hard and fast.

I open my mouth to say something, but he interrupts. "You are mine, treasure." He puts the ruby necklace around my neck.

"Then take me."

He sits up and tugs me to him and guides me so that I half sit on his legs with my back to him, my knees on either side of his thighs. His erection burns my butt cheeks. He plants soft, wet kisses on my back. "Mine," he says against my skin.

He lifts up my thighs and surprises me by pinning me on his

cock. He slides through the slick folds of my sex easily, and I gasp from the fountain of pleasure inside of me. He's stretching me, deep inside of me, and he's not moving, just letting me adjust to him. I convulse around him involuntarily a couple of times, and he groans.

He leans back against a rock. One hand covers my left breast and begins playing with it, his other hand travels to my swollen, aching, throbbing clit, and his fingers begin teasing me. I gasp as intense pleasure spreads through me.

"If you want me to go slow," I moan, "you are doing it wrong."

"We shall see," he growls.

Continuing to play with my breast and my clit, he begins to withdraw, so slowly the pleasure is intensified tenfold. An eternity later, he's thrusting back into me, and I meet his hips as he sends another blast of bliss through me.

He's rocking his hips back and forth, again and again, and I'm thrusting back against him. My body is loving it, and my soul…my heart…are loving it so much it terrifies me.

Yet I can't stop him. He's playing me like a master plays a violin. He's torturing me with the sweetest pleasure there is.

He's going faster, both his hands on my hips now, moving, thrusting me onto him. My breasts and the necklace on my chest bounce, the ruby brushing against my throbbing nipples occasionally, teasing me, sending me to the next level of arousal.

And I'm falling apart. All too soon, the orgasm is building in me. Like the first wave of a tsunami born in the sea, it starts deep. James is getting close, too. He's tensing, going faster. My release is building. There's a pressure and tension inside me, and it intensifies. I'm meeting him thrust for thrust, as my impatience spirals out of control. I can't get enough.

As pleasure explodes inside me, and he's finding his release, I'm opening up to him, allowing his name to caress my lips countless times. We join together in the bliss, the sky, the eternity.

He wraps his arms around me and presses my trembling body to his. As the most world-shattering orgasm of my life is calming down, we are still breathing one breath. I'm leaning with my back against his torso, staring into the endless blue sky and the ever-changing white clouds flying by.

And all I can think of is that nothing in the world can top what I just had with James.

Not jewels, not sex on a volcano, not even time travel itself.

How the hell can I go back to a normal life after this?

But I know I can never stay.

CHAPTER 16

*S*amantha

My body molten, flooded with warmth and softness, my mind high, I absorb the delicious hardness of James's arms around me. I lie on his chest as he cuddles me.

I wish I could stay with James forever.

What I felt just now, being one with him—like he could feel every part of me, and I could feel every part of him, body and soul—I've never had that with anyone. Not even Leonard.

The thought grips my stomach like an icy vise. Memories of the pain and humiliation I felt with Leo rush into me like a cold stream of water. My vow to never allow another man emotional power over me rings in my head: *never, never, never...*

And yet that is exactly what I'm doing.

I'm falling for him, giving him the power to crush me.

You are an idiot! the voice in my head screams. *You are cuddling. Cuddling is for when you are in love. You are not in love. You're just...*

Anger and fear burn me inside, shaking me and sending my body into shivering spasms as though I have a fever. I shake so hard I think the earth is moving.

I push myself off him, the softness, the warmth in my body, replaced by cold, metallic hardness, which closes over my heart like the bars of a prison cell.

I begin to dress quickly, yanking the clothes on, still shaking slightly, feeling as if even the ground is vibrating. I don't look at James. If I do, I'm afraid I'll allow him to change my mind.

"Are you quite finished with me?" he says, his voice broken and raspy. I see him dressing in my peripheral vision.

The words slash me. What an idiot I was to allow this to happen. I don't respond, the metal around my heart that has protected me since Leonard is gripping my throat. Tension is building inside of me. Can I stop shaking, please? I put on the shoes.

"I knew a woman like you would never give me her heart. You only want a man to satisfy your needs," he says. "Anne taught me that lesson. You only confirmed it."

His words cut me. I don't mean to hurt him. I should run—take the necklace now and go.

I finally meet his eyes, feeling as if my lungs are clenched in a fist. His face is stern. His mouth is a hard line. Fury and pain thunder behind his eyes.

"What do you want me to do, James?" I ask. "Stay? Okay, I stay. Then what? I can never be the kind of woman you want. One who only cares about giving birth to your babies and worries about how many eggs the chickens laid this morning. I can't make you happy."

The shaking is over now—it's good that I said all that. And although the trembling tension in my legs is gone, inside I'm hurting, as if a crack has opened in my heart and it's throbbing.

James's jaws clench in a pained grimace. "I certainly had not planned to want someone like you."

"Well, too bad. I've told you I'm not planning to stay." I lean down to take the jade necklace, but just before my fingers touch it, the ground jolts so hard, a loud crack rends the air. The jewels clank, gold coins spill to the ground and roll in all directions.

I lose my balance and fall. With horror, I see the jade necklace slip and land on the ground at the edge of the rock above the lake. Waves splash, and a big one crashes near the rock where I'm plastered.

"Samantha!" James yells as he sinks to his knees by my side and helps me stand up. A barrage of waves assaults us, high and chaotic. The ground rocks, bushes and grass shake.

A wave slams into me, pushing me away from the necklace. And when the water is gone, so is the jewel.

* * *

James

"THE NECKLACE!" Samantha yells, and ice replaces the blood in my veins.

She sinks to the ground, looking into the lake, but the white waves rise high.

The desperation in her face stabs at my heart. If the necklace is lost, she stays with me forever. It seems that destiny might want us to be together.

Should I jump into the water and look for it? I can't let her do that, it's too dangerous. The rock under our feet cracks and stones fall into the lake. Samantha looks back at me, and her eyes are wide, terrified, like a trapped animal's.

If I do nothing, I *will* trap her here. With me.

Do I want to be her jailer? Would I be able to live with myself, knowing that she had wanted so much to go back home, and I had done nothing to help her, pretended like it was out of my control.

No matter how much I want her to stay, I cannot be the one who would trap her where she does not want to be.

I cannot stand her tears, her eyes full of fear. I would rather die.

"Move back," I say as I walk to the edge of the rock.

I jump into the lake and dive down. The waters muffle my hearing, whisper wetly in my ears. The lake is a milky, dirty pool now. Rare water plants waver chaotically as the bottom shakes the lake like a butter churn. I look desperately around the rocky bottom, and there, caught in the crack between two rocks and swaying in the water, is the necklace. I dive deeper, catch it and swim up.

"We must make haste," I say when I am back on the rattling ground. I give Samantha the necklace without looking at her. I cannot bear to see the look of relief she must wear.

She can go now.

I close the chest and put it under my arm, grasp Samantha's hand and tug her after me.

But the mountain rattles and omits another bang. We are both jolted and almost fall but keep each other balanced. The ground beneath us shakes again and a long black crack forms on the other side of the lake. Water from the lake flows into the cavity. There is a loud *hiss*, and steam shoots up from the crack, heating the air around us.

"Come!" I yell and we rush up the hill of the crater.

A scent resembling gunpowder fills my nostrils. Sulfur. Hurrying up the steep hill, with the ground convulsing under our feet, we fall several times. When we reach the top of the crater, an explosion shudders the air, and a hot cloud of ashes and steam hits us in the back. Losing my balance, I pitch back down the hill. The world flashes with flickers of black ground, blue sky, and gray cloud as I roll down. When I stop, my head spinning, my body hurting from the scratches and hits, I lever myself up on my arms to look for Samantha. She is on all fours some distance from me, eyes worried as she looks at me.

"James, are you okay?" she shouts over the rumble of the earth.

I try to stand up, but pain pierces my ankle. I get on my feet, and she hurries to let me lean on her shoulder. The necklace is still in her hand. I can see she intends to guard it with her life.

"Where is the chest?" she says.

I look around and it is down the slope next to a boulder and a stream of water. It is the waterfall we passed by on the way up. Except, the chalice-like rock basin of the pool is not up the slope anymore, but broken on the ground.

"Quickly, come on," she says, and we walk down the slope.

"You must go now, Samantha. Put on the necklace," I say as we reach the chest and I take it under my arm again.

"Out of the question. I need to see that you are safe on your ship first."

"I will be all right. You need to go, right now."

"Forget it, James."

Her worry about me warms me and gives me strength. We step over the stream, which is no longer pure but full of rocks and black sand. As we hurry down the slope, the cloud of ash, smoke, and fumes reaches us and rushes down in front of us.

An explosion hits the air as though it intends to crack the sky open, then another and another. The ground shakes. Rocks, big and small, crumble down the slope, and one almost hits us, but Samantha moves us out of its way. I turn back and look up at the milky-gray cloud of smoke and ash, and within the murkiness glowing red fountains shoot into the sky. A low gurgling adds to it, and my feet freeze as if they've turned to ice. I watch as lava flows through the crack of the waterfall and pours down the slope, mixing with water, hissing, turning partly into black crust.

"Run!" Samantha tugs my hand and I follow her, but I cannot run. My ankle must be broken or hurt badly because the pain is excruciating, and I would surely fall if it was not for her.

The mountain shudders and the crack from which the waterfall originated widens. And inside it is not black—it is glowing red.

More lava is flowing—no longer a brook, it is a stream, and it is quickly turning into a red, glowing river that moves much faster than us. When it reaches the trees, it sets them on fire.

"Come on, James!" she yells into my ear and tugs me after her.

"I will only slow you down," I say. "You must put on the necklace and travel back home. Now."

Her eyes widen in panic.

As the volcano turns the world around us into a red, gray, smoking hell, I calm down. I can't go fast enough to escape this. If this is the end, it must be the end only for me.

Not her.

Because I am in the eye of this storm. And in the calm clearness of that space, I know that I have nothing but love. I love this raven-haired, stubborn, brave beauty who is only a visitor from the future.

Her hair is waving in the ashy wind, her eyes burn darker than the depths of the underworld.

If this is hell, she is an angel, and she will be the last image I see before I die.

I put the chest down, and in one swift motion take the necklace from her hand.

"What are you doing?" Her eyes are alert.

I make a move to put the necklace over her head, but she dodges back. "No, James! I will help you down. I am not leaving you here!"

But as another explosion shudders the ground and above us a new crack is born, there is no time to quarrel.

As she is looking up with horror, I trap her arms around her waist and pull her against me. Her face is panicked. Tears glisten in her eyes. I put the necklace over her head and kiss her.

For the last time, the heaven of her mouth welcomes me, and if I die in the next minute, it will be with the taste of the love of my life on my lips. She answers, desperately, hungrily, and I taste salt on my tongue.

The sensation of her lips weakens, I press tighter to hold on to her, but in a moment, I do not feel her anymore.

Still with my eyes closed, I whisper, "I love you."

CHAPTER 17

amantha

THE GROUND DOESN'T SHAKE. A warm, gentle breeze envelops me in the scents of mango, tangerines, and the sea. A dull murmur of voices reaches me.

I'm not on the horseshoe-shaped island anymore. There's no volcano erupting.

And there's no James.

The thought stabs me, and I almost double up. I open my eyes.

I'm sitting in a chair in the City of Pirates Museum. Across the empty hall, the portraits of James and Cole stare at me. Between them, one jade necklace hangs.

I look down at myself and see that I'm still wearing the rags that used to be the jade dress, but no necklace. My arms and legs are scratched and bruised, and my head and face hurt in several places. My throat burns, and I cough.

James tricked me. He saved me at the expense—

My hands grip the carved arms of the antique french chair. My fingernails hurt. Slowly, I find the strength to stand up, and on unbendable legs I move across the hall towards the portrait.

One question pounds painfully against my temples.

Did he survive?

I need to hold on to something because my head spins and my vision blurs as I squint to see what year is marked under James's portrait: "1690—"

Nothing.

What?

My body chills as though millions of icicles prick my skin.

"What does it mean?" I whisper.

I look at Cole's portrait, and see the same years as before. Should I be happy that at least James's year of death is not 1718? Is he somewhere here, in the future? Had he died in the eruption and everyone thought he just disappeared?

I need to find Adonis.

I walk until my legs gain a little strength, then run. I turn the corner of the corridor and fly by the museum visitors, looking for a red headscarf and a snake. Oh, what I wouldn't give to see that snake now...

Outside, the air hits me with the warmth of the heated asphalt and stones. The sea is down the hill. To the left and right a tropical garden flourishes.

And there, in the shadow of a palm tree, stands a small group of tourists surrounding Adonis. The snake slithers around his neck. Looks like he's guiding a tour.

I don't care.

I run towards him and push people away. "Did he make it?" I yell.

Adonis stops talking and raises his eyebrows at me. "Miss, forgive me. As you can see, I am busy."

"No. No, this can't wait. I just came back. I need to know if

James Barrow made it away from the eruption. There's no date of death. What happened to him? How did he die?"

Adonis narrows his eyes at me, and the snake moves towards me and flickers its tongue. Its black eyes are impassive.

"Are you sure you would like to know?" he asks.

"Yes!"

I know people are staring. I must look like a beggar from the eighteenth century. I don't care.

Because as my heart thumps against my chest the iron bars that I had put there years before begin to melt. James sacrificed his own well-being, his best chance of escaping death, to send me back to safety. He cares about me. My hands are shaking as I wait for Adonis's answer. Because if his answer is that James died, I don't think I can survive that. I don't think I want to live in a world where James Barrow does not exist.

As the protection I had put around me melts away, love floods my system in a warm, sweet stream of joy.

What an idiot. I fell in love with him. I'd rather chop off an arm than let him die.

Which is silly because he must be dead for sure. More than three hundred years separate us. He died at some point.

I just hope that he died in the villa that he had wanted to buy with the treasure, surrounded by children and grandchildren that the woman he married gave him.

The woman I hate.

The woman I want to be.

"Well?" I say. "What happened to him?"

He glances around the group of tourists who are all staring at us pretty much with their mouths open.

"Some think," Adonis says, "he found a mysterious woman who helped him get to the ball, but that he died during the hunt for Cole the Black's treasure."

I clutch the fabric over my stomach. The snake coils a little on Adonis's shoulders and flicks its tongue.

"Others say," he continues, "he got the treasure, but the hunt left him so disfigured he was unrecognizable."

My mouth goes dry, a painful knot forming in my throat.

"Finally, there is another rumor that says that he fell in love with a woman who traveled through time, but she abandoned him, and he never found happiness again."

My eyes blur and burn.

"He realized that marrying a woman he didn't love would never make him happy, no matter how safe she was or how many children she gave him. And if he couldn't settle without the love of his life, he wouldn't settle at all. He gave up the treasure to his crew and went on traveling the world. Some say, he crossed the whole world trying to find a way to her but never succeeded. We do not know when he died, but we know he didn't die a happy man."

While I listen to him, hot tears crawl down my cheeks, leaving burning trails on my skin. My hands tremble again, and I hug myself to stop them.

"A woman who traveled through time?" says a woman, who looks to be in her forties, with a southern accent. She looks me up and down, then takes a picture of me with her smartphone. "I'll be damned. This is a cool interactive theater setup from the museum."

Hope, terrible hope is tearing my chest apart. I don't dare believe what Adonis is saying. I think I know where he is going with this, but I can't allow myself to really believe that James fell in love with me as I did with him.

And yet, he endangered his life to save me.

Leonard would have never done that.

I crossed three hundred years and let a man like James slip away into nothingness? The bad boy who looks like an angel and has the heart of a hero?

"Which of these three legends is true?" I ask.

"Which do you think?"

I keep silent. I'm afraid to really believe, to let the last of the iron protection around my heart fall off and crumble into dust.

To open up to love.

"Doesn't matter what I think," I say. "There's nothing I can do about it."

"Are you sure about that?"

I just wanted to know if he was okay, but none of the answers tell me that he was. In all three scenarios James didn't end well.

Now I know. There's no happy ending for him there. Not without me.

But is there one for me, here, without him?

I look around the group of tourists. When I was in the eighteenth century, less than a day had passed, but it felt so much longer. It's strange to see modern clothes, buildings, cameras, and mobile phones. But that's what awaits me—my job, my apartment, my money.

Continuing my lifestyle where I run away from real human connection because I'm scared to death of allowing myself to be vulnerable.

And I don't see a future here where I'd be looking for a man, planning a wedding, and buying a house in the Hamptons.

My stomach twists, my heart aches so hard it must be turning itself inside out.

Thinking of a world where James doesn't exist turns every cell of my body into dead matter. Does he feel like that, too, back in the eighteenth century?

Would I feel like that every day of my life in New York, alone in my beautiful apartment, working my dream job?

"What are my options?" I say. "What I can I do?"

"You could go back."

"The jade necklace?"

He looks at the snake and smirks. "Yes. But this time, there's a price."

I swallow. "What price?"

"It might be forever. There is no guarantee you can find the way back here. Plus, the obvious. Your job, your apartment, your family and friends will worry."

I grasp my skirts. "Oh my God. How could I have forgotten. My family, my friends… Wait. What about Lisa? Did she travel back to Cole?"

He doesn't answer, just chuckles softly. "That is the price. Do you want to pay it?"

My heart, my body, my soul scream yes.

But my mind…

"That's a big deal," I say. "I have to know I can return if I need to."

"You are a coward, after all," he says. "You just pretend to be strong. You are still looking for a guarantee. There is no guarantee. There will never be a guarantee. You can either live a full life, or a half life. You cannot live both."

My throat clenches hard, my eyes burn, pressure squeezes my scalp. He's right. James showed me what it is to be brave. He's living a half life because he let himself fall in love with someone who told him she wouldn't stay with him. Someone who would rather live a half life than risk her heart.

Anger at myself rises in me. New York, my apartment, and meaningless one-night stands are all a half life.

No more.

What I had with James was a treasure. The full life with him is a treasure.

"I choose a full life," I say, and even though my voice is low, my decision is as hard as iron. "I want to go back to him."

He gives a nod and gestures for me to step away from the group and follow him.

While we walk, I ask again, "What about Lisa? Is she here?"

"She's with Cole," he confesses.

I shake my head. "You bastard. You sent her back, too? Then I guess it's good I'm going back. I must find her."

He chuckles.

When we're out of earshot, he says, "You need to hurry. You must put on the necklace. James will make an important decision soon, and if you are not next to him, you will never see him again."

CHAPTER 18

ames

I WATCH *Sea Prince* float away into the horizon. The sun is up high. Behind me, Nassau smells like hot stones and mango and failure. My twisted ankle burns slightly under the heated trousers.

My hair is cropped, and I'm wearing a hat and a black patch on my left eye even though it is not hurt. I am a wanted man by the British Empire, and I must leave New Providence Island as soon as possible.

I wait for a man called Dirty Jim who will take me with him to the East Indies, as far away as possible from the island where I so stupidly fell in love.

With that thought, my whole body hurts more than it did when I fell down the volcano crater.

But I hold on to the thought because that memory of

Samantha is better than no memory at all. I close my eyes and recall her scent, her silky skin under my palms, her voice as she teased me, defied me, and as she moaned from pleasure.

After discovering what I felt with her, I cannot possibly consider marrying a woman I do not love. All I can do is run. Run to try to forget Samantha. Run to find a new goal in life. Run away from here, so that the pain of never being able to see her again does not flatten me like a fly.

"Are ye Bennet?" says a screechy male voice behind me.

I turn around. An older sailor stands before me. I stand up and pick up my bag.

"I am," I say.

"Come, then, and make haste. The cap'n did not want to take another passenger. Ye have something for him?"

I nod and clap my bag. I kept a large jade stone and three gold coins to buy passage and some supplies. The rest of the treasure I gave to the crew and retired as captain. They were mainly good men who had been at sea too long. They proved their loyalty in the end when they did not abandon me upon seeing the erupting volcano but risked their lives to come and save me.

It gave me so much joy to see the eyes of my men as they received their shares of the treasure. Now those who wanted to retire could afford to do so, whereas others could continue their adventures or even buy their own ships. Or just live like kings until they spent it all on rum and women. Finally making my crew rich healed something in me and brought a feeling of satisfaction.

While we walk along the shore that borders the last buildings of Nassau, I think I see a raven-haired woman between the houses. *Samantha!* my heart shouts. But that is impossible.

I turn away and continue towards the harbor.

Men are throwing provisions into a rowboat, and my

companion informs me this is our crew and I am to join them. I throw my bag in there and join the men who are hefting casks with water, biscuits, and dried fish. My leg hurts, but it will be healed soon enough.

I need to build a rapport with the men I am going to spend months in the same ship with.

When I hand a cask to a sailor, I hear quick steps of someone running. Instinctively, I shove the cask to him and spin around, my hand on my cutlass. A woman with raven hair flying in the wind runs towards me in a ruby-red dress that looks so expensive it is fit for a queen. She is too far off, and I am blinded by the sun. The woman reminds me painfully of Samantha, but I do not dare believe it is her.

"Excuse me," she says as she reaches the first sailor on the jetty. "Have you seen James Barrow?"

When he shakes his head, she goes to the next one. "James Barrow?"

Shock covers me, blinds me, makes my throat convulse. I want to believe what I think I am seeing, but that cannot be. I have sent her away. I have seen her disappear.

Then I finally understand what unravels before me. The voice is hers. The hair. The build and height. I put the cutlass back in its sheath and walk towards her, my gait stiff, limping when I use my injured leg.

By some miracle, she is here.

"Samantha," I say when I get close enough, and she turns her head to me.

Her eyes widen. "James," she mouths and flies into my arms.

I take her and kiss her and engulf her, pressing her to me so hard I might crush her. Her mouth is hot and soft and velvety. Her taste makes me hard. It really is her.

"My jewel," I say when I lean back to look at her. "Why are you here?"

"I had to make sure you were all right." Her big dark eyes shine but cloud with worry when she looks me over. "What happened to your eye?"

I chuckle. "Nothing. I must disguise myself here."

She looks at the boat that is still being loaded. "You were leaving?"

"To the East Indies."

"So I'm not too late." She smiles, then a frown creases her brow. She slaps me on my chest. "How could you do that? Put the necklace on me like that?"

"You know why I did it. You needed to go. So I made you go."

"But I wanted to get you to safety first."

"I am safe."

"How did you escape the eruption?"

"I found a stick and used it for support. I hurried down as best I could. And when I could not go any farther, my crew came to find me."

She sighs with relief. "Thank God. You had no idea how much you frightened me. When I went back, your date of death was unknown. You changed me, James. I know it's crazy because we only met yesterday, but you showed me what I can be when I'm not afraid to be hurt. I was a coward, hiding behind the facade of a woman who does not care about intimacy. But when I felt what I felt with you, I couldn't imagine living without it for a moment. So I came back. I don't know what the future holds, James. But I know I want to find out with you. So I came to stay. For now. Maybe forever. I know my adventure with you is not over, and as long as I love you, I want it to continue."

"You love me?" I whisper. My heart is twisting and opening, and it is sweet and aches as if a magical balm has begun to heal a bad wound.

"I do."

"Did you not say you never wanted to love anyone?"

"I did."

"And yet?"

"And yet I love you."

"My heart has been full of you since I saw you. I just did not want to allow myself to believe that you would not betray me. But you did not. And you showed me that I can love like I have never loved before."

She kisses me again. Tenderly, slowly, as if we have nowhere to go.

And we do not.

"Hey, Mr. Bennet!" a man says from the boat, and I break the kiss and look at him. "Are ye coming or are ye staying with yer molly? We are leaving."

I look at Samantha. "I'm staying," I say to him without breaking eye contact with her. "And this is no molly. She's a lady the likes of which you will never see again."

I am rewarded with the brightest smile of my life.

"Waste of time." I hear the man mumble and the jetty shudders as my bag lands by my feet. The boat sets off.

"I need to get off this island," I say. "There is a price on my head."

"Right. I might have an idea of what we could do."

"What?"

"We could find Cole. My friend Lisa must be with him."

"But he is in the East Indies, is he not?"

"No. I know for a fact he's somewhere around New Providence Island. And I got a clue on how to find him."

I smile, my chest fills with light, warm air. "An adventure then?"

She smiles back. "An adventure."

Samantha kisses me. And as our lips meet and meld together, the feel of her pressed to me sets my blood on fire. But even though she thinks it will be an adventure finding Cole, she has no idea that the real adventure will be spending every day with her, no matter what.

THE END

READY FOR COLE and Lisa's story? Keep reading in your favorite store now.

JOIN THE ROMANCE TIME-TRAVELERS' CLUB!

Join the mailing list on mariahstone.com to receive exclusive bonuses, author insights, release announcements, giveaways and the insider scoop of books on sale - and more!

ENJOYED THE BOOK? YOU CAN MAKE A DIFFERENCE!

Please, leave your honest review for the book.

As much as I'd love to, I don't have financial capacity like New York publishers to run ads in the newspaper or put posters in subway.

But I have something much, much more powerful!

Committed and loyal readers.

If you enjoyed the book, I'd be so grateful if you could spend five minutes leaving a review.

Thank you very much!

ABOUT THE AUTHOR

When time travel romance writer Mariah Stone isn't busy writing strong modern women falling back through time into the arms of hot Vikings, Highlanders, and pirates, she chases after her toddler and spends romantic nights on North Sea with her husband.

Mariah speaks six languages, loves Outlander, sushi and Thai food, and runs a local writer's group. Subscribe to Mariah's newsletter for a free time travel book today!

- facebook.com/mariahstoneauthor
- instagram.com/mariahstoneauthor
- bookbub.com/authors/mariah-stone
- pinterest.com/mariahstoneauthor

Lightning Source UK Ltd.
Milton Keynes UK
UKHW012156230522
403390UK00002B/423